# Like a Fox

## Judy Mitchell Rich

# Contents

# Acknowledgements

I am grateful to friends and family who read and reread this novel, giving feedback, advice, and encouragement: my sons, Matt and Mitch Todd; writers' group members, Paige McRight, John Bush, and Joyce Pettis; my friend, colleague and excellent editor, Houston Hodges; Barbara Rex; Miriam Winter, who gave me valuable information about St. David's Day; sisters Susan Bryan, Sally Mitchell, and Rebecca Cartier (all of whom gave me help with medical matters); and sister Kate Murray who answered my questions about music. Thanks to my cousin Bob McDonald who brilliantly coined a new genre especially for me, Ecclesiastical Forensics. Thanks to all of you who have encouraged me.

*To the parishioners of*
*Emporia Presbyterian Church,*
*West Campus*
*Who taught me about our shared Welsh heritage*
*And still celebrate St. David's Day*
*the first Sunday of March each year*

# KANSAS, 1987

"You're really going to do this, aren't you?" Suzanne's husband asked. They stood in the garage behind their cars, having hugged Peter and Julie and waved them off to school.

"Yes, I am. Did you think I would change my mind on the first day?"

"I wish you would. You'll come crying to me before the year is over."

"Bell, do I ever do that?" She craned her neck up and tried to stare him in the eyes even though he stood a foot taller than she did.

"No, I guess not, but I can tell when you're hurting. That last church you served—." He shook his head. "It turned out okay in the end, but I can't help thinking how dangerous it was for you and the kids. From what I hear this church is much worse."

She continued to stare, torn between irritation and affection. His clerical collar accented the handsome face she had fallen in love with in seminary, and after seventeen years of marriage, he still had the football player's shoulders. Beer had taken a toll on his belly, and his hair receded more every year. He complained about those things, but they didn't matter to her. She loved him steadily, even though the last year since their move to Kansas had put a strain on the whole family.

He opened the car door for her and kissed the top of her head, messing up her hair, which she had so carefully rolled into a twist to give herself some height. She gritted her teeth and got in. As she backed her car out, she muttered, "I may be short and blond, but I am not a child."

* * *

Suzanne drove on automatic for miles of straight, flat roads. Few cars and trucks interrupted her increasingly anxious thoughts. The autumn prairie grasses had turned a bison-color. Their gentle waves reached all the way to the horizon and engaged her preoccupied mind for a moment as she traveled east from Salina forty miles and then south for twenty more.

Suddenly, the tollbooth appeared out of nowhere. When she rolled down her window to pay, the smell of cinnamon rolls beckoned her. She drove slowly watching for the bakery and looking for street names that matched her directions.

I deserve coffee and a roll before facing this church, she thought, as she passed the Holiday Inn, the Texaco station, and Comfort Inn, but saw no bakery. The aroma intensified. Her stomach growled. At the next intersection a huge factory spread out on her right, not a cozy bakery but Hometown Bakery Products. After another two blocks a different aroma fought with that of baked goods. It was steaks. No, maybe beef stew. It grew more intense than that, stronger, heavier. Her stomach rolled. Middletown Meat Processing appeared on her left. The bakery and meat odors mingled in a god-awful smell. She gave up the idea of coffee.

Her disappointment pulled the remainder of her self-confidence into a long thin line of dread. An hour earlier she had been curious, even excited about the challenge. I felt like I could take on lions and tigers and bears. Powerful, that's what it was, she thought. I felt powerful. But maybe that was simply pride, my ego inflated from helping Harvest Church survive. But I think this is a call from God. I really think it is.

Nobody had encouraged her to take on this troubled situation. "You've been warned," her husband Bell had said. "I hope they don't destroy you."

Yes, she had been warned. Even Dr. Talley told her, "Steel yourself, Suzanne. From what I hear, they've run off the last three pastors." As executive for the Presbyterian churches in northern Kansas, he wanted her to go there but was honest enough to say, "I don't think the Lord himself could save that church."

She had phoned the church's previous pastor. "We called them 'clergy killers' in seminary," he said. "I'm the third one who's left the ministry because of them. My advice is don't sacrifice yourself. They are terribly abusive."

"What kind of abuse?"

"Verbal and emotional, nothing physical—though I wouldn't put it past a couple of them. Insults, rumors, sabotage. I still can't believe people in any church would act like that."

When she told Bell about that conversation, he said, "Suze, I'm not opposed to you working. Heaven knows we need the added income, but you've paid your dues. Let's find something that's worthy of you. Besides all that, it takes almost an hour to get to Middletown.

"I know, I know, but there are no other churches available. I'm lucky the Presbytery has asked me to be their traveling interim." She paused, glad and a little surprised to see him concerned about how far away she'd be. So often she felt superfluous to his daily life. He went to his office in the morning and had meetings many evenings. Then when he got home, he sat in front of the television.

"Bell, those people are in a mess, and I might be able to help. Anyway, they can't all be abusive."

"You are so stubborn," he said. "I know you get all passionate when anybody's hurting, but think about it. I know the United

Methodist Bishop. I could ask him if they have a church closer to us that's looking for a good associate. They'd take a Presbyterian."

"I don't want you begging for a job for me, Bell. God help me, I'm going to do this."

* * *

Turning left and grateful to be further from the stomach turning smells, Suzanne found her way through a neighborhood of dark green lawns and wraparound porches. And there it stood, Covenant Presbyterian Church. The long building stretched out low and then strained into a peak.

The serene setting didn't fit her image of a troubled and abusive church. Eyes still focused on the beautiful building, she pulled her briefcase out of the back seat at an awkward angle and banged her hand against the car door.

Rubbing her hand and taking a deep breath, she fixed a smile and prepared herself to face hostility.

At the top of a flight of stairs was a tripod holding a sign. "Welcome, Pastor Suzanne." A note was taped to the top of it.

"Pastor, I've gone to the post office. Your study is through the door to the left of my desk. I'll be back soon. Liz (your secretary)."

She passed a copy machine and the secretary's desk and peered through the door. Now, that's a pastor's study, she thought. Empty bookcases filled two walls, a round table in the middle of the room held a bouquet of gold chrysanthemums.

The desk backed up to a large window. She pushed and pulled the desk to move it perpendicular to the window, then slipped her shoes off and sat down in the high backed chair. It reclined and a footrest popped up. Now, she had a view of the expansive green lawn and a glimpse of the peaked roof.

She jumped up. I mustn't be found lounging on my first day. She roamed the room with pleasure then saw beside the flowers a rectangular gold box. "Welcome from your elders," the card on top said.

Chocolates. They sure know the way to this woman's heart, she thought, letting one of them melt in her mouth.

The outside door clanged shut. "Yoo hoo."

Suzanne slipped into her high heels and pulled her suit jacket into place before meeting the woman outside the secretary's office.

"I just couldn't wait to meet you. Am I the first?" Though white haired and stooped over, the woman exuded energy from her Nike shoes to her bright blue eyes.

"You're the first," Suzanne said and held out her hand.

The woman offered a two handed shake. "I'm Mildred, Mildred Owens," she said. "We're so glad you're here. We'll become great friends. I'm sure of it."

The door opened again and a thin, muscular young woman leapt up the stairs two at a time. "I just knew you'd come while I was gone. So sorry I wasn't here to welcome you. I'm Liz, your secretary. I see you've met Mildred, and did you find your office? Here, let me put the mail down."

She put the box of mail on her desk and surprised Suzanne with a big hug. "Welcome, welcome. Did you see your flowers?"

"They're beautiful, what a nice surprise."

"They're from the Women's Association. And the candy is from the elders who are on the Session right now. We just elected new ones, but plenty of time for all that later."

"Have you had a chance to look around?" Mildred asked.

"No," Suzanne said. "I've only been here a few minutes. Will you show me?"

"Come on, Liz. Play secretary later. Let's give the grand tour. We'll start with the sanctuary. You won't find a more beautiful one anywhere."

Suzanne stood at the double doors taking it all in. Long rows of dark walnut pews sat on a stone floor, and a blue carpet covered the wide center aisle leading to the chancel. It looked to be a mile away, the front wall rising four stories to a peak.

They left the lights off, and as they walked down the aisle in the dark sanctuary, Suzanne admired the stained glass windows on the side walls. Their biblical scenes contained many colors, but shades of blue dominated; and morning beams, glancing through the windows on the left, brushed deep blue over the pews.

"Sacred space," she whispered as they moved quietly toward the front. The pulpit stood high on the left side. A lectern on the right held a large Bible, and an eight-foot long communion table sat front and center. On the wall behind the table a gold stylized cross curved upward into the height of the steeple, flanked by two long and narrow stained glass windows.

"See how the left windows have symbols of baptism and the right ones have symbols of communion?" Mildred said. "The ones down the side walls of the sanctuary are scenes from the Old Testament on the left, New Testament on the right." She reminded Suzanne of a magician's assistant the way she danced around and pointed. Liz sat in the front pew looking up to the peaked ceiling.

Suzanne examined the front windows and the silver chalice on the table and then climbed into the pulpit. Five steps led into a three-sided box. "I've never preached from so high," she said looking out into the dark at the long aisle, the blue haze and shadowy pews.

Liz and Mildred led her to the parlor, which held antique tables and chairs and a grand piano. They showed her the classrooms in the educational wing and then, on the lower level, the fellowship hall which held round tables and a kitchen.

"We made this kitchen big enough for twenty women to do up a meal." Mildred said.

* * *

Alone in her study, Suzanne stared at the boxes of books they had helped her unload from the car. Her thoughts whirled as she popped another chocolate into her mouth. She hadn't expected a warm welcome. Her shoulders relaxed, and for the moment so did her resolve to be strong and invincible.

She found pictures of her former churches and stood them on a book shelf. Third Presbyterian in Longmarch, a large brick church near Chicago, sat looking stiff and proper. She and and Bell served as co-associates there for three years. The second was an A frame neighborhood church in Columbus, Ohio, where she was pastor for seven very happy years. And the third was Harvest, a little white frame church sitting in the middle of wheat fields south of Salina. That was her first Kansas church and like nothing she'd ever experienced before. Now, a second year-long interim lay before her. She could remember lessons learned at each church and people she'd met who had become like family. I hope that happens here, she thought, but heaven only knows what I've got ahead of me. She unpacked the quilt the Harvest women had given her and spread it across the round table.

Liz peeked in the door. "I forgot to tell you. Your computer will be here tomorrow. It's being cleaned up."

"Liz," Suzanne said, "I didn't think you would have computers. Most churches I know continue to debate about getting them. And I have to confess that I don't even know how to turn one on. Maybe I won't need to learn. I've heard they don't really save you any time, and you can lose everything you've been working on. Anyway, I brought my electric typewriter and will probably be more efficient using it."

"Pastor, I know they're scary. We wouldn't have one except a secretary at the college replaced hers last year and gave us the old one. Imagine that, a second computer when most people don't even have a first one. I'm still learning. I've moved our membership and finance files onto the computer, but I still keep paper files, too, just in case. Let me teach you some basics and see what you think. It's amazing what it can do."

Over the next few weeks, she proved to be a patient teacher. "You don't have to hit a return arm or key to tell it to move to the next line. Just keep typing, and when the words reach the margin of your page, they automatically start on the next line. You can also "Cut" and "Paste." This is a mouse, the latest thing. It moves that little arrow on the screen wherever you want it. If you want to move a sentence from one place to another, click down on the mouse and move the arrow over the sentence. See how it makes a shadow over the words? Then let up on the mouse clicker. You can click on cut to remove that sentence, and then go to where you want it, like this, and click on paste. Voila! It appears there magically. And, you'll love this, if you make a mistake just go back and type over it. To get a printed copy, go here. When you read it, if it's not right, go back, change it on the screen and print it out again. No more carbon paper, no more erasing or whiting out mistakes."

Suzanne learned quickly and agreed the computer was miraculous. With Liz close by and willing to answer questions when she got stuck, she began to get comfortable with it.

However, every time she began relaxing into her new environment, she reminded herself to keep her guard up. At any moment she expected to trip over the hidden roots of the church's troubles.

# CHAPTER 2

THAT first week Suzanne called a meeting of the current elders with the intention of making a plan of action. They sat around the library table, fidgeting and looking as anxious as she felt. She opened the meeting with a prayer and in order to get acquainted asked each one to talk about his or her favorite hymn. The four women and five men participated readily, relieving some of her anxiety. No one balked at her leadership or challenged her.

"I'm pleased to come and work with you all. My style is not to change you into some image I have of a church. I take seriously the Presbyterian way of partnership. You elders are ordained because we believe you're called by God and selected by your congregation for a particular ministry. We are partners in leading this congregation.

"I plan to begin by observing the congregation's life and listening carefully to what you have to tell me. My office door will be open to anyone who wants to come in and talk. And I will count on you to communicate with me any concerns or situations that need my attention. Of course, I also will depend on you to attend to your committee's area of the church's life. Let me know when you are meeting, and I'll try to be there, at least at first.

"My plan right now is to concentrate on names and then seek to have a significant encounter with each member over the next several months. I'll start with shut-ins and those in nursing homes. At our meeting next month I will let you know how that is going and we'll decide what's next. Do you know of anyone in the hospital?" They looked at each other, but no one offered any names.

After the committee reports, she opened the floor for remarks and new business, but no one spoke up. She reviewed her proposed schedule with them: office hours Monday through Thursday 8-4; Friday and Saturday at home; Sundays all day for worship, visits, and meetings. "Of course, I'll be on call at all times, and we can have evening meetings as necessary. If we need to adjust, we can do that as we go."

There was no sound. Their faces all looked to her to go on. I hope this isn't going to be one of those sessions, which is quiet during meetings but makes decisions in the parking lot afterward, she thought.

Maybe that wouldn't happen. They observed *Robert's Rules of Order*, even making a motion and a second before discussion. And they addressed her formally as Madam Moderator. Most church sessions she'd known had a folksy style and didn't even observe the rule of waiting to be recognized before speaking. Having an accepted structure and process already in place for meetings should help her lead them through any conflict.

"At the next meeting I'd like to discuss your finances and how you're organized. Do you have a budget, a mission statement, manual of operations and personnel policies?"

Heads nodded. Bronwen Lewis, the Clerk of Session, started flipping through her minutes for the documents. Her husband John pulled out a copy of the budget. Liz's grandmother Anna found their manual of operations.

After graduating from seminary Suzanne had firmly believed that a pastor could organize a church into peace and effectiveness. It had happened in Ohio. Her small, failing church had grown well the seven years she served them, and she had left them with a plan for yearly renewal. However, organization didn't work at her last church in Harvest. They knew nothing about how to be an organized church and that wasn't what they needed. On the contrary she learned a valuable lesson from her time with them: First love the people. Covenant church may need both organizational tuning up and love, she thought. And who knows what else?

After the Session meeting, Morgan, the youngest elder, hugged her. "We're glad to have you here." Her long denim dress and single braid down her back set her apart. In contrast, the others wore business attire and shook her hand before they left.

As Suzanne drove home that evening, twilight gave way to an engulfing darkness broken only by her headlights; a sliver of a moon; and stars, which inscribed patterns on the sky. Suzanne felt her shoulders relax.

* * *

On her first Sunday, Suzanne looked out at the scattered individuals in the pews. She wondered who among them had caused trouble in the past and who would be a challenge for her.

They sang hymns with energy, accompanied by the excellent organist, Diane. The choir director, Jewell, expressively conducted twenty men and women on the anthem. A buxom alto sang wistfully, "I lift my eyes to the hills. From whence does my help come?" And the choir responded, "My help comes from the Lord, Who made heaven and earth" in a rising tide of praise and joy.

Suzanne thought her sermon message unnecessary after that inspiring anthem. And she began by saying so, repeating the words of the Psalm. Then she illustrated it with stories and various ways of reframing and applying the Word of God for that day. "The beginning of wisdom is the acknowledgement that we need God. When we speak that need and when we are patient for the answer, we will find clarity. As you and I begin this pilgrimage together, let us be clear that we need God to lead us and keep us on the right path."

The people in the pews looked as though they were listening attentively, and they laughed readily. She didn't see any scowls or eyes which avoided her during the sermon except for one man who sat in the last pew, chin on chest through the whole service. He stayed seated and didn't participate in the liturgy. She thought he must be ill.

Toward the end of the sermon she left the pulpit and walked to the aisle by the first pew. The man way in the back looked up. "I may never do this again," she said. "The pulpit is good to hold onto. But I want to be closer to you this morning to talk about what our worship time together will be like. We will focus on what is most important, our need for God, our love of God with our whole being and loving our neighbors as we love ourselves. Our worship will be a time of sanctuary, and if you have past conflicts with anyone here, please leave those on one of the shelves by the front door. We will make this a time of personal healing and spiritual growth. Together we will be still and know that God is with us. My hope is that you will consider this a place of refuge, a time of peace for you and for each one who enters this room."

\* \* \*

On her second Sunday, Suzanne stood at the door shaking hands. "Bronwen and John Lewis," a woman thoughtfully reminded her. Suzanne recognized them as elders on the Session, Bronwen the clerk and John the treasurer and finance chairperson. They looked like a matched set, a wedding cake couple who had grown into their tailored suits and touches of gray in their hair.

"We'd like you to come home with us for dinner today if you're free," Bronwen said.

\* \* \*

Suzanne found their home east of the city in the rolling hills near the community college. As she approached their street, she noticed that houses sat barely within eyesight of their neighbors. A few thin trees, with brown leaves falling, strained to reach upward. It looked to Suzanne as though they pretended to protect their houses. Trees in Kansas always looked puny to her, never reaching the size of the pines and oaks in Ohio and Alabama.

She still missed Ohio and the church she had to leave when Bell lost his job as Director of Christian Charities and decided to go back to being a pastor. It was her turn to follow him, but it landed them a twelve-hour drive away from everything familiar.

Nevertheless, after a year, Bell had settled into First Presbyterian Church in Salina, and she had completed one interim pastorate for the Presbytery. The children, Peter and Julie, had adjusted fairly well to their new school. At thirteen Peter had the most difficult adjustment, but Julie had managed well, perhaps because she was a year younger. The two children tended to get along well. However, her own relationship with Peter continued to be strained most of the time. She thought his outbursts of anger came from resentment about the move, but Bell said it was normal teenage breaking-away behavior.

She turned into the long, steep driveway and smiled at handsome horses flicking their tails and grazing on the hill to the left. On the right, in front of the Lewis house, stood a huge metal sculpture, black with red oxide. It looked like a rearing horse made up of all angles and attitude.

As the Westminster chimes played announcing her arrival, she reminded herself that these were parishioners, not social friends. She needed to be cautious until she learned what lay underneath the serene surface of Covenant Presbyterian Church.

The moment Suzanne had waited for came midway through the meal. "Every church has problems, don't you think?" John said.

Suzanne nodded, ready to hear what they thought, but Bronwen cut him off abruptly, asking if anyone wanted seconds.

The conversation had flowed easily as they got acquainted. They now knew that her husband Bell was pastor at First Presbyterian in Salina, and that they had two children, twelve-year-old Julie and thirteen-year-old Peter. With interest and gentle questions they encouraged her to give details about her college in Ohio, meeting Bell at seminary in Chicago, and their vocational paths, which led them from Illinois to Columbus, Ohio, where she pastored a church and Bell did social service work. Suzanne stopped short of describing how painful the move to Kansas was for Peter and Julie and how much she grieved leaving her thriving church in Columbus.

Suzanne asked polite questions, too, and found out that John taught psychology at the Community College and Bronwen taught art at the high school. They had known each other since kindergarten.

"Are these your paintings?" Suzanne asked Bronwen. From the dining room she could see a huge canvas in the living room, an extreme close up of a calla lily, its curves protecting the upward straining pistil and stamens. Another oil painting hung on the wall she faced. It looked almost as though the young woman in the picture had a place at the table. She bent over a rosebud and looked up through long lashes, laughing with delight. Light flowed over her pink cheeks and flashed from her huge brown eyes.

"Yes, that's our daughter Rose. She died at a young age. Come," she said standing up, "let us show you the rest of the house."

Suzanne had never seen anything like it except in magazines. Palm trees and ficus stood between the living room and floor-to-ceiling windows. Beyond them Suzanne saw a landscaped lawn and a swimming pool. Plush white carpet covered the sunken living room floor. She waited, thinking they would take their shoes off, but when they didn't, she followed them down four carpeted steps to the long, white couches, which hugged three sides of the square. Silk pillows of bright jewel tones overlapped each other on the couches.

The pillows matched the colors of five teardrop pendants hanging over the dining table. And those same bright colors appeared in the kitchen on the seats of barstools pulled up to a counter facing a window the length of the kitchen.

Suzanne noticed Persian carpets at the entrance doors. Surely no one would wipe their feet on those, she thought.

"Come, see the lower level." Bronwen directed her down steps covered in the same white plush, and Suzanne wondered how a child had ever lived there.

It was no typical basement, but looked as luxurious as the main floor. Comfortable chairs snuggled up to a fireplace, and a television covered most of one wall. Suzanne was cold. Had she known them better, she would have suggested they light a fire and sit there a while.

"We want to offer you this for when you need to stay overnight," John said showing her the three bedrooms and two baths.

"There's room for the children, too, you see," Bronwen added spreading her arms wide. "You could have this whole level to yourselves. We'd love to have you use it."

Suzanne wondered if it was her imagination, but it seemed like the first time she had seen a genuine smile from Bronwen. "Oh, my, that's very generous of you. What a beautiful home." It was tempting, but she had a nagging suspicion she shouldn't accept favors from anyone. "I'll let you know if we need it."

\* \* \*

The first weeks went by quickly. Suzanne kept waiting for the abuse, but it didn't come. To the contrary, many expressed gratitude for her preaching and worship leadership. And no conflict showed up at any of the committee meetings she attended. She wondered if maybe a group of troublemakers had left.

"Liz, have many people left the congregation in the past year?"

"No, nobody except those who died or moved, but it's rare for anybody to move away."

She asked Liz for the worship attendance numbers and found that numbers had fallen off during the three months between their previous pastor leaving and her coming, but now, there were more in worship every week.

Perhaps I should ask Liz about the conflicts of the past, she thought. But I don't want to stir anything up by asking the wrong person. For now I'd better watch and listen carefully. Eventually, I may trust someone enough to give me objective information.

# CHAPTER 3

MILDRED Owens, ever present at the church, flitted around on Mondays tidying up after Sunday. Other days she was available to go to the post office or whatever Liz or Suzanne needed. She provided a friendly welcome to anyone who came in the building. If the only thing the person needed was a reprieve from loneliness, Liz and Suzanne could continue with their duties.

Mildred told Suzanne several times that people were thrilled with her ministry and wanted her to stay and be their pastor. Suzanne repeated the same stock answer every time. "My ministry is specifically to be your interim, helping you get ready for the next chapter in your church's life. I'm not permitted to be your installed pastor."

After several times of that, Mildred began asking, "When can your family come? The women want to have a welcome meal on a Sunday as soon as possible."

Bell couldn't find a Sunday he could miss worship, but finally the personnel committee agreed on a day when he could leave Salina immediately after his sermon. He and the children arrived in Middletown just as Covenant's later worship service ended. As Suzanne shook hands at the door, Julie stood nearby close to her dad, and he put an arm around her. Peter slumped against a wall and looked at the floor, hands in pockets. He had wanted to stay home, but Bell insisted he go along.

Mildred led them to the church basement and past the food. Bell's eyes opened wide when he saw the two long tables holding a colorful array of fried chicken, pork roast, meat balls, sweet potatoes, corn, green beans, and layered gelatin salads. On a table off to the side sat pies, cakes and other desserts.

Bronwen, Clerk of the Session, was in charge. She seated them at a rectangular table, obviously a place of honor as it faced the room full of round tables. It was a festive sight, all the white tablecloths had centerpieces of small jack-o-lanterns holding votive candles.

John and Bronwen Lewis sat at the head table with them. And when everyone had found a seat, Bronwen announced, "We have gathered today to welcome Pastor Suzanne, Bell, Peter and Julie into our church family. Pastor, we're glad you've come to be with us and look forward to getting to know you and your family better."

John asked the blessing over the food.

*God our Father,*
*Bless this food that it may give us*
*Strength for the tasks ahead of us.*
*You will all men to be saved*
*and come to the knowledge of your truth.*
*Send the brotherhood of your people out*
*into your great harvest*
*that the gospel may be preached to every creature,*
*and your people, gathered together by the word of life*
*and strengthened by the power of the sacraments,*
*may advance in the way of salvation and love.*

Bell bumped her arm, a signal that he noticed the masculine language.

"It's an old Welsh blessing," Bronwen whispered.

26

* * *

As people finished eating, they began visiting, and the conversations rose from gentle murmurs to loud and raucous talking. Two men claimed Bell, and the three of them walked off, talking about fishing. Young people surrounded Peter and Julie, and they moved like a school of fish to the back of the room. The next time Suzanne looked they were gone.

They came back later, all smiles and bright eyes. "Mom," Peter said, "they have a choir for kids our age. It meets on Sunday afternoons and then they have a youth fellowship meeting. Can we come with you on Sundays and stay until you're ready to go home?"

Julie interrupted him. "Mom, this is Sarah. We're the same age. We were even born on the same day. And her brother is Peter's age, but not born the same day. Peter and I want to come with you on Sundays."

"We'll discuss it with your dad later." She hadn't intended to have the children come with her, fearing their exposure to an abusive congregation. But she had experienced no problems yet. To the contrary, the people couldn't have been more welcoming and friendly.

Bell agreed with the children. "Let them go with you on Sunday mornings. They can do their homework in the afternoon and stay for youth choir and fellowship. They've started to feel at home with the young people at Salina First, but let's let them do what they want to. Besides, I'm not home much on Sundays so if they're with you, they won't be alone. Let's give it a try. If things get hot in Middletown, we can change the plan.

"I like the people," he said. "Maybe you're not going to have any trouble after all. More than one of them said that everybody adores you."

"Adore." The word rang like a warning bell in her ears.

# CHAPTER 4

As if the welcome lunch had broken the dam open, a steady stream of individuals stopped in Suzanne's office during the week. They told her about other pastors with varying and contradictory descriptions: "preached too long," "cold and unfriendly," "more of a teacher than a preacher," "the best pastor we ever had," "had his hand in the money." This didn't surprise her. She knew that distorted information often comes out of churning storms of disagreement. However, conflicting stories left her without any clear picture of their history. Maybe they simply need to tell their stories, she thought, and then they will lay the past to rest and move on.

One woman, Betty, inched into Suzanne's office behind her walker, her face in a perpetual frown. She carefully moved her considerable bulk to a chair at the round table and arranged herself. She smoothed back escaping strands of her white hair. "I want to know when we're going to get a real preacher," Betty said.

Suzanne looked across the table into her gray eyes. "Betty, I'm a real pastor, and I'll be here for at least a year helping you get ready for the next chapter in your church's life."

Betty folded her hands on the table. "I don't understand why we're paying you what we paid Dr. White. He was here all the time. You're way off in Salina, and you're not here all week."

"I'm working an average of 48 hours a week and will come immediately if you have an emergency, Betty. If something can't wait an hour, Rev. Baumgardner at First United Methodist has agreed to fill in until I get here."

"Well, I don't like it. They ran off Dr. White—said he was never in the office so I don't think it's fair for them to be okay with you not being in the office. I will never forgive them for getting rid of him," she said through clenched teeth. "They spread terrible rumors and ran him off. Now those same people like you even though you're not in the office. Dr. White visited my husband Jack every day that last week before he died. I couldn't have made it through that terrible time without him. And such a beautiful funeral he preached for Jack." She teared up and looked out the window, far away. "Dr. White was a saint. Lots of people agree with me. Some haven't come back yet, but they will tell you the same thing if they do."

"Betty, how long were you married?"

"Fifty-five years."

"Such a long, long time to be together. And when did he die?"

"It was five years ago. I miss him so much, but people tell me I have to move on."

Suzanne handed her a box of tissues. "Yes, grief makes some people uncomfortable, but I've found that no two people grieve the same. It takes as long as it takes. I can't imagine how hard it is after being married that many years."

Betty sniffed and dried her eyes.

"As far as what has happened in the past. We can't do anything about that now. But I'm here to be your pastor." She paused. "Is there anything you need from me?"

Betty's eyes opened wide. "Oh, no, no, there's nothing I need." Suzanne held her walker while she stood up and positioned herself to leave.

* * *

John Lewis brought in the church's financial books to bring her up to date on the church's funds and budget projections. "Looks like we'll come out close to even as long as we don't have a major building problem," he said. "And as long as people keep giving as they are."

Suzanne nodded. "Thanks for making this clear. Do you know who gives what?"

"Yes," John said. "Liz and I are the only ones, though I guess everybody knows Tommy is our main benefactor."

"Tommy?"

"My brother. Some people call him "The Colonel." I guess we never talked about him when you came to dinner. But you may have seen him here. He sits in the last pew and always slips in late to church then leaves early. Tommy's much older than I am. His mother died and my father married again."

"I have noticed him in the back pew a couple of times but not lately," she said. "Do you mind telling me how much of the load he carries?"

"Not at all. Roughly sixty percent of our income is from him."

"Sixty! That's dangerous to have one person giving that much."

"I know, but we'd be sunk without him. And it's been this way as long as I can remember."

\* \* \*

Bronwen came in one day without her usual fixed smile. "I want to talk with you about the children," she said. "They aren't learning what they should. Nobody's teaching them the Westminster Catechism, and they are going to need to know the answers to those questions. I don't understand what could be more important than that. I've mentioned it several times to Anna and her Christian Education Committee, but they pay no attention to me."

"What is the chief end of man?" Suzanne asked grinning, attempting to help her relax.

"Man's chief end is to glorify God and enjoy him forever," Bron-

31

wen responded. She sat stiff backed across the table from Suzanne, and her rote answer didn't reach her eyes. They held no joy.

"That's my favorite question and answer from the catechism," Suzanne said. And the only one I remember, she thought. "Do you find the questions and answers of the catechism still helpful to you on your journey?"

"Oh, yes. Anytime I begin to wonder or doubt, I go right back to them. They settle my mind."

Suzanne smiled at this woman whom she had never seen without an abundance of makeup. That eye shadow, blush, false eyelashes, and stiff updo must take over an hour to arrange in the mornings, Suzanne thought. I wonder what's beneath the shell she presents to the world.

"Bronwen, when I was in high school, my Sunday School teacher taught us the catechism, but then went back through each question, and that time he wouldn't let us answer by rote. We had to use our own words to show we understood what we were saying."

"Oh, well, I guess that's one way to teach them," Bronwen said. "I'll mention it to Anna."

"Bronwen, that picture you painted of your daughter is beautiful, especially the light in her eyes. Tell me about her."

She acted as if she hadn't heard Suzanne. Her eyes glazed over, and she left quickly.

\* \* \*

Suzanne found Mildred arranging hymnals in the sanctuary one Monday morning. "Mildred, I need help sorting out the ministers you've had, their names and the dates they served. It should be in the Official Record Book, but Liz can't find it anywhere."

"I have it at home. I've been checking through it to be sure she's kept it up to date. But I don't have to look to tell you what you want to know." She rattled off names and dates and her summary of each one's life. Suzanne grabbed a pencil and a piece of paper from the pew and took notes.

- *Dr. Davidson, 1945-1965, the best pastor we ever had.*
- *Rev. Mason Terry, 1966-69, he didn't last long. That man had his hand in the money.*
- *Dr. Lee Haupt, 1970-1973, terrible preacher. He left to teach at University of Kansas. He had a drinking problem.*
- *Dr. Robert Roberts, 1973-1982, a dream of a pastor, from Wales, loved to hear him speak. The young people made too many demands on him and drove him to an early death. In the middle of a sermon, he just keeled over.*
- *Brian White, 1983-1986, I won't even call him 'Reverend'. He didn't deserve it. Couldn't preach, couldn't teach, wouldn't visit, had a few favorite people. The Colonel called him 'Wimp' to his face.*

"My Mildred, you have quite a memory. I'll make a list for Liz, too. And I'd like to see the Record Book. Would you bring it in tomorrow?"

\* \* \*

Liz looked over the list. "I remember Dr. Haupt. He did my mother's funeral. I remember Dr. Roberts' Welsh accent, but he didn't relate to young people. Our last pastor Rev. White was great. He started taking the youth group on mission trips. But something went wrong after a while. I lived in Topeka at the time."

Suzanne wrote all the information she'd gathered in her notes; however, except for the names and dates, it added up to a mishmash of opinions and impressions.

# CHAPTER 5

"I hear my grandmother invited you to go with her to the women's meeting at Bronwen's." Liz said one morning, while she opened the mail.

Suzanne waited at the copy machine as it whirred and rolled, making extra finance committee reports. "Yes, she'll be here soon. You know, she looks so young for her age, I'd have thought she was your mother, not your grandmother.

I know. At 80 she should look older than she does. But she's always looked young for her age. In some pictures my mother looked older than Grandmama."

"You must take after Anna," Suzanne said. "You two look a lot alike." They both wore their hair in pony tails, Liz's coal black and her grandmother's black with only a touch of gray. And they both had youthful faces, long and narrow with high cheek bones. "Your eyes have the same glint of humor.

"I see that in Buddy's eyes, too," Suzanne said. "Last week he asked me if I knew who Michael Jackson was. When I said 'Yes, he's one of the Jackson Five,' he rolled his eyes at me. He said, 'No, he's the one who does this.' And he did some kind of backward walk."

"I don't know how Grandmama does it," Liz said, "but she keeps up with that kind of thing. I sure am blessed to have her taking care of Buddy while I'm at work. He's at the age where he soaks up knowledge and information like a sponge. And Grandmama is a match for him. She teaches him a lot and gives him good experiences. He gets more exercise with her than he would with me, too. They walk all over town. She's always been one to walk anywhere she can instead of driving. She used to run. But three years ago she had both knees replaced so now she's walking, not running, and Buddy and I can keep up with her better."

"She's very intelligent, isn't she?" Suzanne asked.

"She's always been a big reader. She went to the Teacher's College here. That's what the Community College was back then."

"Are you talking about me?" Anna called from the outside door. Buddy came running up the steps and into the office to give his mother a big hug.

"Of course," Liz said nuzzling his neck. "We talk about you and Buddy all the time when you're not around."

"Pastor Suzanne, are you ready to go, schmooze with the women?"

"I'm ready. I hope you'll help me remember their names."

"Sure, I will. Let's get going. Bye bye, Buddy, I'll be back in a little while and we'll go home and fix that surprise supper we were talking about. She winked at him. Bye, Liz."

\* \* \*

Bronwen welcomed Suzanne and Anna and showed them to her elegant dining room. About two dozen women held coffee cups and chatted there and in the sunken living room. Anna graciously introduced Suzanne to women, as though she hadn't met them, or she gave her names ahead of approaching groups.

When Anna was stopped by someone, Suzanne spotted Jewell and headed in her direction. On the way she heard Mildred's unmistakable syrupy voice. "I just don't know why we have to suffer through those hymns nobody knows," she said to three women. Then she spotted Suzanne. "Well, here's our pastor now. Let's ask her." The three other women looked embarrassed, but Mildred went on. "We were just wondering who picks the hymns."

"I choose ones that fit with the scriptures and sermon of the day. Why do you ask?"

"Well," she said carrying the word out into two long syllables. "We don't know those hymns and it's torture to get through them."

"Oh, really," Suzanne said. "We'll have to look into that." She greeted the other women, making cheerful small talk.

At the end of the meeting, the president asked if Suzanne would like to say a few words.

"Thank you," she said. "I am glad to get to know some of you better. I appreciate you reminding me of your names. I'll go home and study the church's picture book until I know all of you. As I have been enjoying your cheerful gathering, I've wondered how you would put into words what is it you like about Covenant church? What is it you tell people when you invite them to come to worship with you?"

After a long silence six people spoke up. One said, "I tell people about our history." Another mentioned the beautiful building and stained glass. The others mentioned St. David's Day, the women's group, and the music. Then one kind soul said, "I tell people they should come hear you preach. I really appreciate that I can understand what you're talking about and you always give me something to take home. I think about it all week."

On the way home Anna said, "That was a good question to ask that group. They tend toward complaining. I've read that complaining is one way women have of exerting power. Another is manipulation."

Suzanne laughed. "I've never heard that, but it sounds insightful. By the way, I've been meaning to tell you how much Peter and Julie are enjoying your Sunday school class. I think they're just the right age to learn about the theme of covenant throughout the Bible."

"I thought it was a good way for them to get a sense of the whole

Bible," Anna said. "It did that for me back when one of our pastors offered an evening class.

"Suzanne, at that first meeting when you told the Session you were going to observe for a while, I pictured you standing off in a corner making judgments about what was going on. But I see that you are not at all aloof, and it seems to me that the way you meet people is unique. I suspect you don't realize it, but like today—. What is it I'm trying to say? Um,... your interest in each person seems to me to be genuine and up close and personal. I think maybe what I'm seeing is an extraordinary ability to love people even before you get to know them. There should be another word besides 'observe' for what you're doing."

"Oh my, Anna. Oh, my." Suzanne was stunned. "I'll think about that. I hope it's true."

When she told Bell about the conversation, he said, "That's quite an astute observation on her part. I think it's true. It's probably why people tell you their life stories. They never do that with me."

"You're more interested in social service and social action," she said. "I've always felt guilty for not being as active as you are."

*  *  *

Other than individuals reliving their anger, grief or joy over previous pastors, Suzanne experienced only good will and friendliness at Covenant Church, and she began to entertain the idea that perhaps the previous three pastors had been as abusive and incompetent as various members told her.

"It's a dream church," she told Bell. "Do you think they could have had three ill-matched pastors in a row?"

"Highly unlikely," he said.

She knew he'd say that. And he was probably right, but she was having a wonderful time getting acquainted. She enjoyed getting to know a church's unique personality, its quirks and secrets. It reminded her of putting together a jigsaw puzzle. In a short time the individuals and the whole congregation transformed in her mind from random bits of information and impressions to a full color picture, a three-dimensional one that walked and talked, even though in a church the puzzle pieces tended to bump into each other occasionally and change the picture.

* * *

The children began going with her on Sunday mornings and staying for the evening youth choir and fellowship. While Suzanne made visits in the afternoon or worked at her desk, they sat in the library and did their homework.

Soon their friends Matthew and Sarah Edwards began to join them in the library until youth choir and fellowship meetings in the evening. Their family was very involved in the church. Their older brother Robert was the regular youth choir director; although, their mother Jewell had been filling in for him while he got started as a freshman at Middletown Community College. Jewell was also the adult choir director, and she and Ed led the youth group.

Suzanne enjoyed planning the worship music with Jewell, a lively pink-cheeked, round woman, full of life. It seemed that when she stood to direct, her light lit up the faces of the choir.

One Sunday Jewell invited Suzanne, Peter and Julie to join her family for dinner after church. It was a brisk, snowy day but Matthew and Sarah stood on the front porch waving as they drove up. The red door distinguished their house from the other two story, frame houses on the street.

"Look, they found extra sleds," Peter said. And he and Julie ran off before Suzanne could get to the front porch.

"Go on in," Sarah yelled over her shoulder.

Jewell Edwards called from the kitchen, "Come on back here, Pastor. I'm stirring and can't leave the stove."

Suzanne made her way to the kitchen, stepping around boxes of board games and a deck of cards spread out on the living room floor. "Smells marvelous."

"Caramel cake. This is Ed's birthday so we're having his favorites: pizza, salad and this cake. I'm so glad you could all come. We'll do it again when your husband is able to join us."

"I didn't know it was a birthday dinner. We should have brought something." Jewell stood at the stove, and Suzanne sat down at the table, which stood at one end of the long narrow kitchen.

"I didn't tell you for that reason. You'll make this more special for being here, so don't think any more about that. Ed will be here soon. He's downtown at his shop making his birthday portrait. You know he's a photographer? Every year he documents what he calls 'his growth.' He also does it for each of us, whether we want him to or not." She glanced at Suzanne out of the corner of her eye and grinned.

"Now, I'm going to put the cake over here by you, and I won't tell if you just happen to get some on your fingers." Her bright blue eyes danced.

When the pizza arrived, so did the children along with Robert and his dad Ed. They gathered at the dining room table and Robert prayed, thanking God for the good man who was his father. He ended with a song that the others joined in singing. Even Peter and Julie knew it, an upbeat version of the Doxology.

"Praise God from whom all blessings flow, (clap). Praise God all creatures here below, (clap). Praise God above ye heavenly hosts. Praise Father, Son and Holy Ghost."

Ed entertained them over dinner with riddles. "Which weighs more, a pound of feathers or a pound of bricks?"

Sarah said, "Well it has to be the feathers because these riddles are always what you don't think they'll be."

"No, not feathers. What do the rest of you think?" Ed asked.

"Bricks," Peter and Matthew said in unison.

"No, that's not right."

After they discussed it a long time, he looked to Robert.

"I know the answer, but only because you already pulled that one on me. They both weigh the same. A pound of anything is a pound."

There were arguments and groans. Sarah was not convinced. "If you drop a brick and a feather from a window, the brick will hit first."

Peter tried to explain the logic of it, but she wouldn't give in.

When they finished the birthday cake, Robert said, "Dad, in honor of your birthday, the twerps and I are going to clean up, wash the dishes, and wrap the cake." His eyebrows wiggled up and down at his mother in an imitation of his father.

"Oh, great," Jewell said. "The very night I use paper plates. Now, you save that cake for your dad. I know how you wrap up a cake."

"And then," Robert went on, "I challenge you all to a ping pong tournament."

\* \* \*

Jewell and Suzanne took their coffee into the living room and sat looking out the front window. Wet clumps of snow clung to every bush and tree.

"How long have you lived in Middletown?" Suzanne asked.

"All my life. Soon after Mother and Dad married, they moved here. Dad taught psychology at the college. They've both gone on now. Ed's folks, too. Our parents were good friends and loved to tell stories about how they knew Ed and I were meant for each other from the time we were babies in the church nursery."

Squeals from the basement interrupted them and Suzanne's mother ears perked up. Then the regular hollow bounce of the ball on the table put her at ease.

"John Lewis teaches psychology, too, doesn't he?"

"Yes, Dad was his mentor. I think John was as crushed as I was when Dad died."

"If you've been here all your life, you must know everyone at Covenant Church."

"Oh, yes. Oh, yes. Many good friends. Some have been like brothers and sisters." Her voice cracked, and a cloud overshadowed the light in her face.

Suzanne debated with herself whether to ask about it. But then Jewell went on.

"I guess you know that some have had a falling out."

"Yes, I've heard that but I've not seen any sign of it."

"People are trying to be good, I guess. Seems like they always start out that way."

Suzanne sipped her coffee and admired the snow scene then realized Jewell was wiping away tears.

"I don't know what has happened to us. We used to be so close, but now some have stopped speaking to each other."

"Has that happened to you?"

She pulled out a tissue from up under her sleeve. "A person who has been like a sister to me for years won't talk, won't give me a clue what's wrong. She won't even take my phone calls. I miss her so much, and I can't figure out what I've done to drive her off."

They were interrupted by children screeching as they chased each other up the basement stairs and through the living room. Suzanne tucked away the knowledge of Jewell's pain for a future conversation.

"It's time for youth choir practice," Robert said. "To the car, squirts."

"I'll go, too, Jewell," Suzanne said. "Your family sure is busy on Sunday with Robert leading the youth choir and you the adults. And then you go back in the evening for youth fellowship, too. I'm grateful for all you do. Now, I'll let you and Ed have a few minutes

42

before you meet with the young people. Thank you for inviting us. We sure did enjoy having dinner with you all."

What a nice family, Suzanne thought as she drove back to the church. They're definitely part of the twenty per cent who do eighty per cent of the work. The church is blessed to have them, and I am, too. I couldn't ask for better friends and influences for Peter and Julie.

# CHAPTER 6

THE Monday before Thanksgiving, was a chilly, dreary day. Liz poked her head in Suzanne's office. "You've been summoned. Tommy Lewis wants you to come see him at ten this morning. But I need to tell you something before you go." She held up her palm to stop Suzanne. "I heard you tell Mildred that you like to form your own opinions and not hear about people before you meet them, but (and this is a big 'but') there are two things you need to know for your own good before you go over there. Wear your steel toed shoes and picture your spine as an iron rod. The less you say the better off you'll be. And one more thing, get there exactly on time, not a minute early, not a minute late. I'll wait here until you get back."

Suzanne took a deep breath. Summoned? Tommy Lewis. That's the brother of John Lewis, the one who supports sixty per cent of the church's budget and sits in the back pew when he comes. For a moment she considered having Liz call to say the pastor is busy today, but she could visit tomorrow at two. However, her curiosity and distaste for lying won out over her pride.

She went to her study to work on a sermon for Sunday and was deep in thought when Liz knocked on her door. "Time to go. By the way, don't be surprised if Catherine, his wife, calls him 'The Colonel.' Some do. He's considered a war hero."

It wasn't far away, and Suzanne having been alerted by Liz to the importance of punctuality, sat in the car staring at the majestic house, irritated with herself for taking orders. The bricks on the huge house showed their age, but the wood trim was bright white. Sixty seconds before the requested time of arrival, she walked through the gate of a waist high brick wall at the street to a similar gate in another wall of the same bricks which stretched across the front of the house.

Seven stone steps led Suzanne up to a porch. She felt very small beside Corinthian columns, which stood two stories high and held a round wooden canopy.

A maid opened the door before she knocked. The woman wore a severe black dress only one shade darker than her skin. The black was set off with a crisp white collar, white cuffs on the long sleeves, and a white apron. "Come in, Reverend." The woman never lifted her eyes to see Suzanne's smile. "Right this way."

A center staircase, wide and grand, swooped up from the entry hall, its maroon carpet flowing from the front door over wide stairs to the second floor. Walnut bannisters curved up and at the top continued around a gallery landing.

The maid ushered Suzanne into a room on the right, and left her there. Glass bookcases hugged the walls to the right and a large desk sat in front of them. Its highly polished surface held only a formal pen and pencil set in an official-looking medallion. French doors looked out on a secluded garden where bushes were shaped to look like leaping deer.

She turned when the door opened. A withered woman wheeled herself in. Thick silver hair swooped away from her delicate oval face and formed a roll around her head. She wore a gray silk dress, which reached all the way to her footrests. "Reverend Hawkins, Catherine Lewis. Welcome to Middletown," she said in her soft southern accent.

"Thank you. I am pleased to meet you." Suzanne shook her hand and met her weary pale blue eyes.

"Won't you have a seat? Mary will bring tea." She motioned Suzanne away from the window to a chair. "You've spotted my deer. The gardener likes to be artistic, and finally The Colonel has humored me and allowed him to create this garden." Suzanne spotted a mannequin in uniform near the door she had entered. "Is that your husband's?"

"Yes, it seemed like a good way to display his medals."

Suzanne couldn't ask more, for Mary brought in tea, and a towering man strode in behind her. He filled the frame of the door, and his scowl filled the room. She had never met anyone with such a big head. It sat on his thick neck like a cube of limestone covered with a mass of black curly hair. His incongruous white bushy eyebrows spiked out as unruly as his hair.

Mary set down the tea service and guided the wheelchair toward the door. "Time for my medicine," Catherine said. "I'll leave you two to talk."

Tommy held the door for the women as they left, and Suzanne stood to greet him, but he strode heavily around the room and didn't look at her. "Those idiots at the Presbytery cause us nothing but trouble. What are they thinking sending a girl? This church needs a man with *cojones* to straighten it out. What are you going to do?"

Suzanne hesitated, wondering how to respond. Does he want an answer or is he just looking for someone to yell at? Finally, she said, "Right now I'm getting to know people. And this is a good chance to get acquainted with you."

He ignored her. "How are you going to fix the church?"

"Fix it? I am at this point observing and getting to know how this church operates. What do you think needs fixing?"

He snorted. "Trouble always comes when the Presbytery interferes."

47

Even his teeth are big, she thought. They look like pictures of George Washington's dentures, rectangular and yellow. He paced around the room. I'm not sitting down unless he does, she thought. It didn't matter though. At five feet two inches tall, she became a little girl again. Her stomach clenched and her head began to ache.

He opened a drawer of the desk and took a cigar out, cut it off and lit it with jerky movements, then waved it around. "We need to go back to having trustees. We always took care of things, anything that was needed. Now, it's all falling apart."

"Did the trustees and the Session work well together?"

"No leadership. We haven't had leadership since Dr. Davidson. He knew how to preach. He knew how to lead a church. That last yahoo called God 'She.' An insult to God. And now, that damn Presbytery sends us a girl.

"Some of us don't hold with a woman in the pulpit. They should stay home and take care of their families." He looked down at her for the first time and stared in her eyes. "What's your husband doing without you to warm his bed at night?"

Whoa, Suzanne thought. Keep your cool here. Her chest tightened and her face grew hot. Remember what you've been taught. What? What have I been taught? Conflict management tools don't exactly fit. If his criticism were more directed at me, I could ask him to tell me more. But I don't want to hear more of this. She felt trapped and paralyzed. This is how I feel when my dad goes into a rant. Her heart beat faster and breaths came short and shallow, but she tried to appear calm and stand as tall as she could.

As a young girl, she had escaped from unpleasantness at home by finding comfort in the Air Force Base Chapel wherever they were moved. Right now she longed for the peaceful dark sanctuary of Covenant Church and wanted to get back there as soon as possible.

She cleared her throat and pointed to his medals. "Tell me about the war," she said in an attempt to get him to respond.

He stopped pacing and sneered at her, waved the cigar, then strode to the window.

She tried again. "I've seen you in the back pew a few times at church but not lately."

He stood still looking out the window. "I won't be back."

"Tell me, what do you need from the church? From a pastor?"

He grunted but didn't turn to look at her.

"Well, if you need a pastor, I'm here for you. You can call on me."

He turned, waved the cigar dismissively and stomped out the door. Seconds later Mary came in. "I'll show you out, Reverend."

\* \* \*

Suzanne walked out into the drizzling rain, head held high, but stumbled when she reached the road and caught herself on the gate. She passed by her car, hitched her purse up onto her shoulder and walked furiously for two blocks. Such behavior often indicates deep pain, she told herself. Such behavior often indicates deep pain. She repeated what she knew to be true, but the truth didn't enter her heart. By the time she got back to the car, her breaths had deepened and her heart beat had slowed, but her head ached and now she was chilled. She unlocked the car and glanced up in time to see Tommy staring at her from a foyer window. She stared back and then smiled and waved. Kill him with kindness, she thought. He looked away first and disappeared from the window.

On the way home she realized that he might have meant that he was withdrawing his financial support when he said he wouldn't be back.

How could I have handled that better? she wondered. What would Frances have done? Her best friend, a United Methodist pastor in Ohio, could handle aggressive behavior with amazing compassion and firmness. I'll call her. Maybe there was something I could have said—just the right thing to make a connection.

* * *

Liz stood as soon as Suzanne walked in the door. "Are you all right?"

"Yes, and I'm ready now to hear whatever you know about Tommy Lewis."

"Okay, but we've had a death. They're waiting for you at the funeral home. It's Mrs. Miller."

# CHAPTER 7

THERE was no sign out front. She checked the house number against what Liz had written. The Victorian house with its wraparound porch looked like a home children would rush to after school for milk and cookies. But the number matched what Liz had written down, and a man in a dark suit and tie appeared on the porch and waved.

The short, wiry man met her half way up the sidewalk with an umbrella. "I've been watching for you. Our sign's being repainted. I'm John Johnson, the funeral director here." He offered a warm and gentle handshake. "I'm sorry I haven't been around to get acquainted yet. Welcome to Middletown. Let's get you out of the rain."

His professional demeanor and occupation didn't preclude a warm smile and light-filled eyes. "Mrs. Miller's family is here. Did you know her? She lived at The Presbyterian Manor."

"Yes, I've visited her."

"Good, that will make it easier. Her two nieces are from Kansas City. They're her only family. Here are their names and the information you'll need. They're talking about a simple graveside service."

He led Suzanne into an overly warm parlor, which smelled like lilacs and the burning wood in the fireplace. The two women sat in wing chairs by the fire, and John pulled up a chair for Suzanne. He put another log on the fire. "I'll be back in a few minutes to see what you've decided."

The women knew what they wanted, a simple service at the cemetery as soon as possible. One of them had a box of tissues in front of her and a handful of soaked ones. Suzanne moved a waste-basket to her side. The other sister sat tall, and took charge. "Aunt Ida requested the twenty-third Psalm and the song 'Suddenly There's a Valley'."

"Tell me more about her," Suzanne said.

"She was so good to us, more like an older sister than an aunt. She never married and had no children. Aunt Ida took charge of our education. She introduced us to the Nelson Atkins Museum in Kansas City and the KU museums. I always liked the anthropology one. She showed us how to use a library, and she'd take us to the best ones to do our homework. We had resources no one else had. If we were curious about anything, she helped us find out about it."

The other sister talked through her tears and sobs, "She put us both through college. Mother and Dad didn't care much about edu-cation."

"What a blessing to your lives," Suzanne said. "I can see what a great loss this is for you."

"Lately, with this Alzheimer's, it's been like she was already gone. We came to see her every Sunday though." The woman broke down into uncontrollable sobs.

"I've visited her, too," Suzanne said. "She sang 'Amazing Grace' with me one time."

"She did? I'm surprised she could do that. I wish you had known her before..."

John returned and they agreed on the arrangements. "We'll see if Tommy Lewis will sing," he said. "That's what she wanted. But if he can't do it, we'll ask Robert Edwards."

Suzanne finished making notes while John walked with the women to their car. When he came back, they chatted a few min-utes. "Do you mean Tommy Lewis, The Colonel, sings?" she asked.

"Yes, he has a beautiful voice, and he's requested for most of the funerals in town," John said.

"You know, it looks like it's clearing out there. Do you want to grab some lunch at Pete's and talk about how you prefer to do funerals?"

His stride and speed matched Suzanne's preferred brisk pace. They talked the whole way and didn't stop for two hours. Closed casket during the worship as a witness to the resurrection, check. Visitation at the funeral home, clergy usually come early and stay late, check. Funerals usually in the church for members, check. They dispensed with those usual details fairly quickly.

"I have many of your members on file," he said. "I mean if they've told me what they want in their services, scriptures to read, hymns to sing, and other requests. Most of them want The Colonel to sing that song about the valley. Every one of the old Welsh does for sure."

"Welsh?" Suzanne asked.

"Oh, yes. There is a heavy Welsh population here. They came over and worked the coal mines and farmed. My great grandfather came in 1875 from northeastern Wales and settled over near the Cottonwood River. Now, the Colonel's family, the Lewises, settled the same time as my family did. The Welsh have always been the pillars of the community.

"You'll notice that for many of us the first name and last name are similar like mine, John Johnson. And please call me JJ. Everybody does since my dad was John, too. You'll find a Robert Robertson, Tom Thompson and others. They used to have worship services in Welsh, and even now on St. David's Day they sing some in Welsh.

"Very interesting. Now I understand why the church called Rev. Roberts to come here from Wales. By the way, I have Welsh background, too, on my mother's side," she said. "Are you a member at Covenant Church?"

"I think I'm still on the rolls. I contribute and I sing when the

Welsh choir gathers to practice the first of the year. I was real active for years. After Dad died, I got out of the habit of Sunday mornings, what with my work being so unpredictable."

JJ was easy to talk with, interesting and interested in what she had to say. She liked his twinkling brown eyes, so full of humor. He reminded her of Donny, her best friend in grade school. He and Suzanne played together every recess, usually jumping rope although they had to tie the rope to a pipe on the end of the school building since no one else would join them. They called Donny a sissy because he liked to jump rope. He was her first best friend, but that ended when the Air Force moved her family. She wondered where Donny was now and if he remembered those good times like she did.

Suzanne left JJ at the funeral home and drove back to the church. He seems trustworthy, she thought. Maybe eventually I can count on him for an objective account of the problems in the church.

# CHAPTER 8

THAT evening after dinner Suzanne told Bell about her encounter with The Colonel. "I'd have kicked him in his *cojones* if I'd been there," Bell said. He moved his feet off the dining room chair left vacant by Peter and sat up straight. "He had no right to talk to you that way, and he's lucky I'm not in Middletown. You are going to have to take charge of this situation. Be stronger. What did you say when he was so rude?"

Suzanne leaned forward. "Shhh. Julie will hear you." Peter had cleared the table and Julie was in the kitchen finishing the clean up.

"I told him I was there to be his pastor and to call if he ever needed me."

Bell groaned. "I could never do that. You are too, too nice to deal with this man. God help you."

"Do you really think a man like that will listen to a woman confronting him?" Suzanne asked.

"Now that you mention it, I think the woman's husband needs to confront him."

"Don't you dare. That would really cause problems."

"Well, then you have to. Tell him the way it's supposed to be. Teach him how to act. Claim your authority."

"Hmmm," Suzanne said.

"Don't 'hmmm' me. I hate it when you do that."

"Do what?"

"You always say, 'Hmmm' when you don't want to answer a question."

"I do? Hmmm."

He didn't laugh.

"Seriously, I didn't realize that," she said. "It must be when I'm thinking how I want to respond. Bell, I know you'd do things differently. We have very different ways of pastoring. I can't imagine anyone listening to me if I started giving orders or telling them how to act."

"Yes," he said. "I'm more directive. You're more collaborative. Still, in this situation you're in, you've got to be more authoritative."

"I hear you, but I'll have to do it my own way. Authoritative doesn't necessarily mean confrontational. As soon as I get to know them better and establish relationships, I'll have a sense of what is needed and how to approach it."

"Sounds like gobbledygook to me," he said moving to his recliner and turning on the football game. "He's abusive," he called back over his shoulder. "How would you handle it if he treated someone else that way? Collaboratively"?

\* \* \*

She called her friend Frances in Columbus and told her the whole story. "What would you have done, Frances?" she asked. "Have you ever had someone insult you like that?"

"Suzanne, I think you did really well not to kick him where it hurts." As usual, Frances found humor in tough situations. "My impression from what you've told me is that you're lucky he's not passive aggressive. I'd call it aggressive aggressive. I think it's easier to deal with behavior everyone can see. You brilliantly refused to engage in confrontation. I love that you asked him what he needed from a pastor, and I bet that knocked his feet right out from under him."

"That makes me feel better," Suzanne said. "Bell thinks I should have been tougher."

"Sure he does. A man would have been forced into a duel to uphold his pride in such an affront, but you wouldn't last long if you had been aggressive back at him. We women have to be clever and use alternate ways of fighting. You knew that instinctively. And you responded as Jesus told us to. That is ingrained in you, bless your heart."

"I didn't really 'love my enemy,' but I pretended to. Does that count?"

Frances simply laughed. But Suzanne was serious.

# CHAPTER 9

Rain poured down. There was no way to do a graveside service for Ida Marie Miller. Liz dropped Mildred and Suzanne at the door of the cemetery chapel, and they hurried in while she parked the car in the flooded parking lot. Mildred wore a black silk suit with a very short skirt and had on three inch black heels. It was the first time Suzanne had seen her in other than her white Nikes or Sunday's black lace up shoes. Mildred Owens, she thought, how is it you can wear those shoes at eighty when I can't manage them at forty-two?

A grizzled man in his white shirt and black suit took Suzanne's robe and motioned her down the hall. She left Mildred waiting for Liz and followed him into a small office where he hung her robe on the back of the door and handed her a memorial folder.

JJ came in as she was slipping into her robe. "Too bad about the rain. But this chapel makes for a nice place to have a service," he said. "Now across the hall is the back door into the chapel. From there you can enter through the curtain. Here, let me show you." He put a hand on her back and moved her through the door. "Here's the organist. Meet Jimmy Potter." He was already playing but nodded to her.

"Now, this curtain hides the organist. And behind that one over there is the family. They will be able to see you when you're at the podium, but no one out there in the pews can see them." He checked his watch. "You've got seven minutes. Enter when Jimmy finishes playing "Amazing Grace.""

Suzanne peeked through the curtain. About twenty-five damp people were seated, and a few more stood in line to view the body. The casket sat open in the center front.

She looked through her little black worship book. Since we're inside, it feels more like a regular service, she thought. I'd better make this a little longer than the usual graveside one.

The organist began playing "Blessed Assurance" as she invaded the family space to greet the ones she knew and meet the others.

Then it was time. She slipped by the organist and through the curtain as he concluded "Amazing Grace."

JJ and one of his men came forward, closed the casket and placed a blanket of pink roses on it.

That was her cue. "My friends, we gather in the name of Jesus Christ who said wherever two or three were gathered he would be there, too. In sure and certain hope of a promise to eternal life, we come to celebrate the life of Ida Marie Miller. Her lifetime is now completed."

Suzanne told what she knew of her life and what she would be remembered for, including her love of education and her beautiful flower arrangements. Ida had provided them for the church for thirty years until Alzheimer's cut her off from the world.

"We have words of comfort from Jesus in John 14. 'In my father's house are many dwelling places. If it were not so, would I have told you that I go to prepare a place for you? And if I go and prepare a place for you, I will come again and will take you to myself, so that where I am, there you may be also.'

And from the Psalmist: 'Even though I walk through the darkest valley, I fear no evil; for you are with me; your rod and your staff—they comfort me.'"

"Let us pray. Loving God, you have shared Ida's life with us.

She has come from you and now we offer her back into your arms. Almighty God, we commend to you Ida Marie Miller. We commit to you her care, trusting in your love and mercy and believing in the promise of a resurrection to eternal life."

When Suzanne sat down behind the podium, Tommy unfolded himself from the pew and strode up the center aisle to stand behind the casket. He looked like a bass, so it was surprising that when he opened his mouth to sing, he had a clear tenor voice.

"When you think there's no bright tomorrow and you feel you can't try again, suddenly there's a valley where hope and love begin."

She couldn't reconcile this man with the one who was so rude and crude. Nevertheless, the pathos in his voice connected with her soul. She closed her eyes, and the song lifted her up on a mountain of pain before descending into a valley of hope. At the end, there was absolute quiet. Nobody moved, not even Tommy. Tears ran down his face.

Suzanne didn't want to say anything after that, but the people needed a signal to leave. She offered a quiet benediction over them all on behalf of God and slipped behind the curtain to where the family sat. They looked at her with unfocused eyes and murmured their thanks.

* * *

Liz was drenched when she brought the car around. "Let's go to lunch," Suzanne said, "my treat."

At Pete's, Liz and Mildred ordered beef stew, but the town's mingling odors of meat processing and bakery still turned Suzanne's stomach. She ordered her favorite rainy day meal, chicken noodle soup and grilled cheese.

The waitress said, "Pastor that was a real good funeral you preached today."

"Thank you, Lucille. I didn't see you there."

61

"I know how to be invisible, sneak in late and leave early. Can't get enough of The Colonel singing that song about the valley. And he cries every time."

After they ordered, a man behind Suzanne called to Mildred, "Hey, Millie, soft shoe on over here, baby."

Suzanne turned to see a table of four men in suits and ties. Only one was close to Mildred's age so she assumed he had called out. Mildred straightened her shoulders as much as possible and stuck out her chest as she stood and sashayed over to their table on those high heels and executed a little turn before perching on the man's knee.

Liz grinned. "Eighty years old and she's the biggest flirt I know."

Suzanne tried to imagine what white-haired, stooped over Mildred had looked like in her younger years. Her little rosebud mouth would have been popular in the twenties. She was trying to figure out how old Mildred was then when the femme fatale returned.

She put her hand on Suzanne's shoulder, pressing down hard, then swung her hips into the chair as if those knees and hips of hers weren't hurting.

"Mildred, you remind me of a flapper today. I was just trying to figure out how old you were in the twenties," Suzanne said.

"Honey, I was at my best those years. Tommy and I cut quite a rug: the Charleston, the Tango, even the Shimmy. My mother thought such dancing would bring the end of the world, and my dad ordered me to stop doing those... um, let's just say 'black' dances."

Lucille set their food down, and when she left, Suzanne asked, "You and Tommy?"

"Oh, yes, he was our football star, and I was a cheerleader. Oooh, he was so handsome and romantic. I remember him singing one night out in a rowboat on the lake." She rolled her eyes up and then slowly closed them, her wrinkled face glowing.

"He sang beautifully today," Suzanne said.

62

Liz nodded. "He can be so tenderhearted, and then he'll turn around and become The Colonel, almost a Jekyll and Hyde."

"He's a sweetheart," Mildred said. "People don't understand him like I do. He is very generous. I hear you went to dinner at his brother's house. The Colonel built that house for John and Bronwen. And back when Elmer and I had a fire destroy our house, he helped us out a lot, too."

"Tell me about your husband," Suzanne said.

"Elmer, dear Elmer, he died a long time ago. He was only 61. He had cancer a year and a half, poor darling. In the end a heart attack took him. But," she grinned and crinkled up her eyes, "he died with a smile on his face, if you know what I mean."

"TMI, Mildred." Liz held her hands in a time out T, and then answering Suzanne's puzzled face, said, "Too much information. Always too much information."

Mildred giggled.

* * *

Liz dropped Mildred off at her house, a bungalow one street over from the Edwards' home and waited until she was safely inside. "Mildred will never invite you in, and would be embarrassed if you dropped in," she told Suzanne. "She's quite the packrat, never throws anything out. But she can find any newspaper article you want. We should give her a title at the church, like archivist or historian. Sometime when you have a block of three hours, ask her to show you her files and mementos at the church. She has her own little room back behind the fellowship hall."

Liz pulled into the church. "I almost forgot that you asked about The Colonel. What do you want to know?"

"No gossip, please, but maybe you could fill me in on his history. I know he was in the war and has medals, and I met his wife Catherine. Now, today I see his surprisingly tender, musical side."

"After he came back from the war, he married Catherine. They had met in Virginia when he was stationed there. They moved here and bought that house. She came from money. Tommy was mayor of Middletown after the war for a long time, and he held the office of church treasurer all my life until recently. He finally agreed to let his brother John take it over."

They continued the conversation at the table in Suzanne's office. "John Lewis is Tommy's brother." Liz said. "Did you know that?"

Suzanne nodded but Liz didn't seem to notice. She went on, her eyes focusing somewhere above Suzanne's right shoulder. "Let's see. They are step brothers, or no, I think it would be half brothers. Tommy is much older. His mother died when he was in high school, and his father married again. That second wife was John's mother. Grandmother went to school with Tommy. She says the boys hardly knew they were brothers because there was so much age difference, and Tommy was away while John was growing up. Grandmother told me The Colonel was always fascinated by airplanes and went off as soon as he could to join the Army Air Corps. By the way, she says he was never a colonel. Somebody just started calling him that and it stuck.

"But, you know, now that I think about it, I remember a time when John and Tommy were close. It was when Rose was a little girl. They were all close, John and Bronwen, Tommy and Catherine. Rose was the center of their lives. Tommy and Catherine never had any children. John and Bronwen only had Rose. Bronwen and Catherine made her the cutest clothes."

Suzanne got up to close the blinds against the sun shining in Liz's eyes. "How did Rose die?"

"She fell and hit her head. It was tragic." Liz stared off into space. "Do you know about Rose?"

"I saw Bronwen's painting of her. Bronwen said she died young, but she seemed reticent to say any more than that."

"Yes," Liz said. "I've noticed people don't like to talk about her. Did you know she was... different?"

"No. In what way?"

"She was so beautiful you'd never know from looking at her, but when she talked, she sounded much younger than her age. I'm not sure exactly what was wrong, but I think they suspected brain damage from when she was born.

Rose and I were the same age so we grew up together in the church. Grandmother says I was protective of her from the time we could walk. When I was older, probably about twelve, I didn't like her hanging on me, hugging and kissing. She developed early and was a knock out. The other kids made fun of us. I wasn't very protective then, and I still feel guilty about that.

"At some point she started going to a special school in Topeka so I didn't see her except at church and some in the summer, but not much even then because she was always at the lake. She and my mother died about the same time. Mother had cancer. I was fourteen. I don't remember much about that summer."

Suzanne sat a moment trying to take all this in while Liz got them coffee from the kitchen.

"Liz, what do you feel guilty about?" Suzanne asked when Liz sat the coffee down.

"Not protecting her, I guess."

"Could you have protected her?"

"Not really, except I could have handled it better, not abandoned her when people made fun of us."

"At what 12, 13 years old?"

"Yes."

"What would you do if faced with the same situation at this age?"

"I suppose I would know so much better how to respond to the taunts and still be her friend."

"It would be difficult for a young teen to know how to deal with that."

"I never thought of it that way."

"And now you have that sweet boy, Buddy. How old is he?"

"He just turned seven. I don't know what I'd do without him. He's the light of my life."

"You never mentioned a husband. Should I ask?"

Liz sat quietly, one hand over her eyes. When she finally looked up, her eyes held tears and her mouth quivered. "I married Eddie when we finished college. Buddy was born the next year. We were ecstatic, but then two years later Eddie told me he was seeing someone else. I was devastated until I found out it was a man he was seeing. Then I was furious.

"I still don't understand how he could do that to me. Why did he get married if he didn't love me? I'm still angry and confused."

"I'm so sorry, Liz."

"Thanks. You're a good listener." Liz said. "Is that enough history for today?"

# CHAPTER 10

THE Sunday after Thanksgiving, Suzanne, Peter and Julie drove to Middletown through a light rain. The whole world looked gray. It closed in around them: sky, fields, and roads. Julie wiggled restlessly in the front seat. Peter slumped down in the back and covered himself with a blanket even though the day was unseasonably warm. The wind blew harder than usual, and Suzanne had to hold the steering wheel tightly. She had a headache and her eyes hurt, but she had to get herself ready to see people, answer innumerable questions, and lead worship. Shake this off, she told herself. Think of something positive.

"Hey, you two, I've got good news. Your dad and I have managed to get enough time off to go to Alabama after Christmas."

"But Mom, we can't," Julie squealed. "We can't leave our kittens."

"Cats do all right by themselves for a few days," Suzanne said.

"But what if something happens to them? They're so little."

Peter groaned from the backseat. "Mom, we can't leave them. Maybe we could take them with us. Would Grandma care?"

Care, Suzanne thought, would she care? She'd have a cow.

"Ask Sarah and Matt today how to take care of them. They'll tell you how to set them up safely while we make the trip. After all, their cat produced those little fur balls. They'll know what to do."

The wind picked up and blew the car toward the middle of the road. Suzanne gripped the wheel and strained to see through the rain. Up ahead she saw flashing lights and slowed down. A state trooper motioned her to pull over.

"Where are we?" Peter sat up. "What's going on?"

She rolled the window down and rain flew in. The trooper dripped water onto her shoulder from his hat. "Ma'am, we've got a tornado headed this way. Go to the school building two miles ahead and take cover. You've got about ten minutes, plenty of time. Now, move along."

"Mom, hurry, hurry," Julie said.

Peter scoffed at her. "He said we had plenty of time." But Suzanne noticed that he was frantically looking at the sky.

At the one story concrete block school a dozen people hunched into themselves, sitting on the floor in a hallway. Suzanne did the same and watched them for clues about how dangerous the situation was. No one looked panicky.

Peter shared his blanket with Julie. Suzanne took her dress shoes off and wrapped her wet feet in a corner of it. They sat on cold linoleum and leaned back against the concrete walls.

Suzanne's breath came fast and shallow. She tried to slow it down. All she knew of tornadoes came from the Wizard of Oz and tales people had told her. She'd taken cover several times as a child, but no tornado had ever struck near her. Even though people warned her about tornadoes in Kansas, after living there a year she had stopped worrying every time a storm came since no one she knew seemed to take notice. Now the reality of a tornado brought her as close to panic as she'd ever been. It reminded her of being stranded with her mother in an Ohio snowstorm. Suzanne told herself to be strong, not to fall apart like her mother had.

Julie moved closer to her mother. "Mom, what's happening?"

Suzanne put an arm around her and said, "Julie, I'll keep you safe. Stay close to me." I'll throw myself over both children if the storm comes down on us, she thought.

A man sitting next to them wore overalls and stroked his white beard. "Don't worry, missy. Mostly the twisters just blow over, haven't had a bad one around here for a couple of years. And it's rare to have one form in the morning like this especially now we're near on to December—very rare. Course, you can't never count on Mother Nature. She may be waiting to drop one on us when we least expect it."

Peter squinted up at the man. "Have you ever seen one?"

"Sure have. The worst one was in May of sixty-five, tore up my house and barn, and made a swath through the wheat like a harvester."

"Did it look like the one in Wizard of Oz?" Julie asked.

"Sort of. They're wild like that one and unpredictable. Some swerve around with a long tail that looks like a snake. Others look like a wide sheet of dirt from sky to ground."

"I want to go outside and see it," Peter said, looking at his mother.

"Now, you just stay where you are and hope you never do see one," the man said. "You'll feel the temperature drop when the front comes through. Just hope you don't hear the sound of a train. If you do, roll up in a ball and cover your head."

Suzanne couldn't think of words to comfort the children. Her mind jumped around. What if we die today? What if someone is injured? How close are we to a hospital? What will happen at church when we don't show up? I've got to pull myself together for the children. She listened but heard nothing except wind and rain. Then thunder boomed and the roof rattled. Her whole body tensed. The rain poured down hard for a few minutes. Before long a man came in dripping water on the floor. "You can go on now. The danger's over. It went south of us. But keep an eye out in case another one drops."

The children ran outside, but Suzanne held back and asked the man, "How can you see one coming when it's raining like this?"

"You can't," he whispered. "If you hear what sounds like a train coming, get out of the car, get down in a ditch, and cover your head."

That didn't reassure her. Not at all.

* * *

At the church Suzanne took some aspirin and put on her white alb. Since it was the first Sunday in Advent, the paraments changed color to purple. She selected a stole from Guatemala. It brought back memories of the gentle woman who wove it. She had met her in a little village her Ohio church had visited on a mission trip.

She decided to use the stole for the children's time in the service and ask them to identify some of the symbols woven into the cloth. They would recognize the cross and fish and lamb. She smiled remembering the little girl in her congregation in Ohio who insisted that the lamb was a dog. She kept punching at it saying, "Doggy, doggy."

She went to the choir room and had a prayer with them, "Lord, we pray for all those gathered here in worship and those caught out in this storm. Be with us as we listen for your Word and speak and sing for you."

Her head pounded as she processed down the aisle behind the choir. She smiled and talked sternly to herself. Fake it til you make it. A smile is just a frown turned upside down. The congregation will take its emotional cues from the pastor. "Why are you cast down, O my soul, and why art thou disquieted within me? Hope in God."

When the choir sang, she was out of sight behind the pulpit so she closed her eyes and melted into the music.

*Jesu, joy of man's desiring,*
*Holy wisdom, love most bright;*
*Drawn by Thee, our souls aspiring*
*Soar to uncreated light.*

I am so grateful to have escaped the tornado. I hope no one was struck by it. Lord, please carry me through this service and be with all who've come to worship you.

During the sermon, she found herself surprisingly impassioned. "This is a season of watching and waiting. Watch for what is important. As a discipline, consider stopping every hour on the hour, closing your eyes, taking a deep breath, and then asking yourself where you have seen evidence of God's love in the past hour."

She continued to keep sermons positive, making worship a time of sanctuary in which old conflicts were not likely to be triggered. First do no harm, she told herself. Her goal was to bring them together by staying calm and reducing anxiety. Issue-oriented sermons would have to wait until she could find what might unite them in action.

During the last hymn Suzanne's eyes scanned the congregation for who was missing and who might be visitors. She noticed for the first time that Sadie Ross, the new Associate Executive Presbyter, sat in the back, her gray hair fitting in with all the other gray-haired people. She had joined the Presbytery of Northern Kansas staff only the week before to work alongside Dr. Talley. While he continued with executive matters, she would be Pastor to Pastors.

Suzanne had met her on Thanksgiving Day at Bell's church where they had dinner for anyone who wanted to come. Sadie, a warm and friendly woman in her fifties, gave off loving, motherly vibes. Upon meeting her, the first thing Suzanne thought was that she followed the latest advice about how various professional people should dress for their jobs. For women clergy, the word was "dowdy." It was deemed important that they not threaten other women when they spent time with their husbands. Nor dare they dress in such a way that would enthrall men. At least that was the thinking behind the recommendations of those who gave advice to women in different occupations.

Sadie dressed the same both days Suzanne had seen her, a blue suit and white shirt. It may be her uniform, Suzanne thought. That would certainly simplify every morning's decision about what to wear for the day's events. Suzanne wore cheerful colors to hospital and home visits, a power suit for session meetings, something dressy on Sundays, and her black suit or black dress for funerals. A blue suit and white shirt, maybe with a clerical collar, would work for everything.

At the door Sadie invited her to lunch. "I'd love to," Suzanne said, "but I have charge of my children and two of their friends so would you be okay with me ordering pizza? We could have lunch here. They'll be in the library and we can talk in my office."

"That sounds terrific," Sadie said. "It will be good to have some privacy so we can talk openly."

What does she mean by that? Suzanne wondered. Is this an official visit? Has a problem come up? Suzanne was aware that the pastor is often the last to know, and sometimes by then everything is out of hand and beyond recovery. I'm being paranoid, she told herself. Stop that.

* * *

Suzanne gave Peter the money for the pizza and asked him to stay near the door to receive it. She showed Sadie to her office. "Come, have a seat at the table," Suzanne said, slipping off her shoes and hanging up her alb. "Ahhh, it's been quite a morning. We had to take shelter on the way here because of a tornado. Did you come through that bad weather, too?"

"I heard about it on the radio, but it went south of me." Sadie hung her jacket on the back of her chair. "It was a beautiful service, Suzanne. And I'd forgotten how peaceful the sanctuary is. I grew up in a Welsh church which combined with two others to create this congregation."

"When was that?"

"Let's see, I was about eight years old so 1945, I'd guess. Two churches from out in the county and a larger one here in town merged. At first, they rotated the location of where they held worship services. Later, when I was in college, they built this building."

"I didn't know that history. Were all three considered Welsh churches?"

"Yes, although the larger one in town was more liberal and held services in English only. The smaller congregations had to adapt to English singing and preaching. The church I grew up in was so traditional that when my parents were children the women sat on one side and the men on the other. And I remember back when they still sang and preached in Welsh."

"Very interesting, Sadie. My grandmother told me some about our Welsh heritage, but I don't know much except for the love of music she and I shared. She knew some Welsh. Her parents spoke it to each other. She said it was their prayer language. There was a word she used. It sounded like whoo-eel. She said it was what happened when she felt the Spirit in the song, like when she'd get goose bumps."

"I know that word. It's spelled h-w-y-l and you pronounced it exactly the way my mother did It means the spirit that lies behind the song. I feel it every time we sing 'Be Thou My Vision.' We Welsh tend to be emotional especially about our music. But you know that from your grandmother. Is she still living?"

"No, she died a few years back. She was probably the greatest influence on my faith. My parents didn't go to church, but she took me with her. They put a special chair for me near the organ. She played for a Presbyterian church in Alabama for years."

"What a lovely place this church will be for you to enjoy that Welsh heritage. Have you heard about the St. David's Day festival?"

"Yes, a little."

Peter and Julie came to the door with pizza and drinks and served them. Suzanne couldn't help but be embarrassed to introduce her son with the long, stringy hair and the earring. At least his sock hid the tattoo.

Sadie asked, "Peter, Julie, do you come here every Sunday?"

"Yes," Peter said, "we like it here. They have a choir for kids our age and we like the youth fellowship group."

"What other churches have you been a part of?"

Julie said, "We were born in Ohio when Mom was pastor at a church there. Then we moved to Kansas and went to Harvest Church with her."

"We really like that church," Peter said. "Mom, I want to go back to see them. When can we do that?"

Julie went on, "And we went with my dad some. It's okay there, but we have really good friends here."

Peter started backing out the door and pulled on her. "Our pizza's waiting."

Suzanne held out her hands. "Let's have a blessing together."

Julie ran out the door and brought Sarah and Matthew into the room. "These are our friends, Sarah and Matthew. Sarah and I were born on the same day." They politely greeted Sadie and then joined hands.

Suzanne prayed, "Lord, we thank you for this food and ask your blessing on it and on each of us. May our time together be full of your joy. Amen."

The children left, and then Julie came back. "Mom, Matthew and Sarah are going to take care of our kittens while we're in Alabama."

When Suzanne and Sadie settled into eating, Sadie said, "I should give you my spiel about Pastor to Pastors. It is good to be clear from the start. I'm here for you, and I won't be doing any references. Dr. Talley will do those. That way you can be open with me without fear that what you tell me will affect future calls. You know, don't you," she said grinning, "that future churches interviewing you will expect you to have been perfect and had no problems. But you and I also know that's impossible, and hiding difficulties is what most of us do. I think pastors tend to do that out of habit. Their parishioners expect them to be a tower of strength at all times.

"A very present help in times of trouble?" Suzanne said.

"Right. Of course, that is God, not their pastor."

Suzanne laughed. "Yes, I think I'm guilty of encouraging that since I readily move into the role of caretaker wherever I am. It probably comes from being the oldest child.

"Sadie, I feel vulnerable in any church knowing that if I make one misstep early on it can imprint an image in people's minds that's hard to correct. But I feel especially vulnerable in this church. Their conflict has to surface sometime. I know the previous pastors can't all have been terrible, and even though I find myself considering that maybe I am as wonderful as they tell me, I know that isn't real. They use the word 'adore' all too often. And you know the old saying, 'The higher the pedestal, the further you fall.' But I don't know who of these wonderful people is going to rise up and show me what has been going on here to cause so much trouble."

"I understand," Sadie said. "One thing I want to do while I'm here is give you some history of this church that you might not know. Have you ever heard of 'after pastors'?"

"No. After what?" Suzanne dabbed at pizza sauce on her blouse.

"It's a term being used to describe a pastor who comes in after a leader breaches the ethical boundaries of their position."

"I've never heard the term."

"It's actually a new understanding for us. It usually refers to the next leader after a pastor's sexual misconduct, but it can also be other misconduct."

"Do you think what has gone on here is in that category?"

Sadie crossed her legs and leaned back. "Hasn't anybody told you about the sexual misconduct?"

Suzanne simply stared at her. Tommy's face flashed in her mind.

# CHAPTER 11

"L ET'S take a walk," Sadie suggested. "Will the children be all right if we leave them?"

"A walk sounds good. I'll be sure the children start their homework. Let's see, I have some comfortable shoes here in the closet." She looked down. Sadie already had on her comfortable shoes, laced up walking shoes, their athletic genre not very noticeable because they were black. Part of the uniform, Suzanne thought.

The sun shone brightly after the morning rain. Fifty degrees of warmth set the stage for a crisp walk.

"What was the misconduct at this church?" Suzanne asked. "Is it something you can share with me?"

"Yes, as Pastor you need to know about it. The long pastorate of Dr. Davidson ended when he and his secretary decided to leave their spouses and marry."

Suzanne stopped walking. "No one has said a word about that."

"He was the one who brought the three churches together and led them in building this new church. Everyone loved him. After the war, during the golden era of the fifties and sixties most of our churches were growing and thriving and full of children. Youth groups and youth choirs formed, the pews were full. Pastors looked really successful. Davidson stayed twenty years. He is the only pastor I remember from my childhood and youth. And, of course, when he left, no one talked openly about the reason for his leaving. In fact, the church didn't call that sexual misconduct at the time. Now, we regard it as such because we've learned more about the role of power in such relationships."

A cardinal flew in front of them and landed on a bare branch. They paused to admire him and then walked on.

"What is the matter with these clergymen?" Suzanne said. "It makes me so mad I could scream. Don't they know that when they break a sacred covenant like that, it can be destructive to the faith of everyone who has trusted them? We've all been taught about the inequity of power between a pastor and parishioner. It's very clear that a pastor must not get involved with a parishioner in other than a professional, ethical relationship."

"There's more," Sadie said. "The next two pastorates each lasted less than four years. Following that, they called an older man from Wales. My dad was on the calling committee and said that once they heard the pastor's Welsh accent, there were no more questions."

"How did he do?"

"After seven years of conflict—some objected to his heavy handed authoritarianism while others loved his accent and keeping to the old ways—he had a heart attack, in the pulpit. It was quite a shock, and his death divided people. On the one side, the younger people wanted more partnership with the next pastor and less authoritarianism. On the other, the older people wanted the old ways, purity and discipline. They blamed the younger group for the pastor's death, claiming they had laid heavy stress on him.

"Debates about alcohol didn't help any." Sadie paused to look Suzanne in the eyes. "Shortly after the Welsh pastor moved here, my mother says the young women's group sold vanilla to support a missionary. Since vanilla is 33% alcohol, the pastor and the Old Welsh chastised them and put a stop to the sale. You may still hear people refer to that uproar.

"Did you know this whole county was 'dry' until two years ago?

The desire for nice restaurants finally won out. They wouldn't locate in town unless they could have a liquor license. Until then you had to join a private club to have a drink. Anyone could go in and pay a couple of dollars to become a member for the evening."

"You are a wealth of information," Suzanne said. In the house they were passing, three little girls stood in the window dancing as though they were on stage. "Cute kids," Suzanne said as they stood and watched them and clapped, much to the delight of the children.

"I know I'm going on and on," Sadie said, "but there is one more piece of information that applies to all this. The last pastor, Brian White, came after the Welsh one. He had a great personality, pulled people together and began programs and mission outreach. About four years into his pastorate, a woman in the community came forward accusing him of having an affair with her. That was after she discovered she wasn't the only one. He had a church trial and was dismissed from the ministry, disrobed, defrocked. The polite term today is 'stripped of his ordination.'"

"I talked with him before I came here," Suzanne said. "He told me the people were abusive," Suzanne said.

"There is no doubt that these people are hard on pastors, but in his case it's hard to say who was more abusive. It's a matter of record. I heard about this from my family members and the former executive of this presbytery, who has been a life long friend of mine.

"When I got here last week, I looked up the records to be sure I had the facts straight before I came to see you. Dr. Talley identified you as the most vulnerable pastor in the presbytery, given the history of this church, so I wanted to begin with supporting you."

"Do you mean this is the most troubled church or I'm the least experienced?" Suzanne asked.

"There is the utmost confidence in you. The impression I got from Dr. Talley and the Committee on Ministry is that they want to protect you from the 'slings and arrows' of this congregation."

"Brian White said three ministers have left the ministry because of this congregation's abuse."

"That's a little misleading, but it's become the common impression about this church, especially after Brian said it often enough. In truth, they've been very hard on their pastors, and they earned the title 'clergy killer church,' but it's incorrect to say three of them left the ministry. Rev. Terry did. And Dr. Haupt had several unhappy years here, but he is still ordained. He did leave parish ministry though to teach The Philosophy of Religion at the University of Kansas. Dr. Roberts died, perhaps as a result of the stresses of trying to pastor these people. And then Brian was stripped of his ordination.

"There are probably several issues so knotted together that I doubt anyone will ever untangle it all. But I believe that they will show their deepest need for healing as they relate to you. If you can walk through that mine field with them and make it to the other side, a domino effect of health may come and give them confidence for the future."

They walked on in silence. The sidewalk ended and a field of wheat lay beyond the last house. "I haven't seen much wheat around here," Suzanne said.

"No, we're in the Flint Hills. They're too rocky to plant, but here and there are a few places with enough soil. That's a nice looking field."

"I like seeing the rows of green like this in their parallel lines," Suzanne said. "But then I think the wheat is beautiful at every stage.

"You've given me a lot to think about," Suzanne said. "It's all quite valuable. Do you have more information about 'after pastors'?"

"Yes. I'll mail you a paper on the subject. Basically, people exhibit a lack of trust in the next pastor, to the extreme. They may question nothing and then suddenly want to know how much you work, how much you are paid, and what you're doing after hours. It can be crazy-making. At first their way of dealing with conflict is to try to eliminate it. 'Zero level,' I call it. Avoid differences at all costs. They may refuse to make decisions or make them too quickly, trying to be agreeable."

"Yes, I've seen some of that, Suzanne said. "Do you have any advice on how to deal with it?"

"Intuition helps and a non-anxious presence is necessary. Personally, I would avoid coming on strong, and I'd try to get them to discuss decisions without anxiety."

"Keeping it at the level of a problem to solve," Suzanne added.

"Yes, that's it exactly. So you know about the levels of conflict. That will help."

Suzanne nodded.

"Teach them those levels."

"Maybe we can practice on something non-threatening."

They reached the church, and Suzanne saw Mildred leaning against her car, arms crossed.

"Thank you so much. Thank you for coming, Sadie. The woman waiting for me is Mildred Owens. Do you by chance know her?"

"I'm not sure."

After Suzanne introduced them, Mildred carried on a monologue about those she knew from Sadie's family. Finally, Sadie said, "Well, it's time for me to go. A hot bath will feel good after that walk."

"A bath?" Mildred said. "I never take baths. How can you stand to bathe in your own dirt? I have to take a shower and let it all go down the drain. Baths always seem so, so. . ."

"Self-defeating?" Sadie laughed. "If I didn't take a bath every day, my hips and knees wouldn't work at all." She waved over her shoulder as she quickly walked to her car.

"Pastor Suzanne," Mildred said, her forehead wrinkled and her rosebud lips pursed as though she had tasted something sour, "is that woman from the presbytery?"

"Yes, she's the new staff member working with Dr. Talley. She is our Associate Executive Presbyter and Pastor to Pastors."

"Is something wrong? Why did she come?"

"No, nothing's wrong. It was simply a friendly visit to get acquainted."

"You know, don't you, that every time the presbytery gets involved, we have terrible things happen to us. You can't trust them. Mark my words. You can't trust them. The Colonel will not like this—not at all."

The sun hovered near the horizon and glanced gray and frosty across the parking lot, the brief warmth of the afternoon gone. Mildred left, and Suzanne hurried back inside. I'm sick of hearing what The Colonel won't like, Suzanne thought. I wonder if anyone cares besides Mildred.

At her desk, she pulled out the list of people she wanted to get acquainted with and considered how many she could visit before the children were through with their youth fellowship meeting.

The phone rang. "Covenant Presbyterian Church, Pastor Suzanne."

"Pastor, this is Middletown Memorial Hospital. One of your members has been admitted, Catherine Lewis."

Great, she thought. I have to go deal with Tommy again. I swear with my hand on the Bible, I will never ever call him 'The Colonel.'

# CHAPTER 12

TOMMY paced in the hallway outside his wife's room.
"What's happening?" Suzanne asked.

"A stroke. They won't let me in the room, and nobody's telling me anything. In five minutes I'm going to call the hospital administrator at home."

Suzanne walked beside him down the hall and back trying to figure out what to say. She wanted to give him comfort, but she was wary. She didn't want his anger spit all over her.

Suzanne stopped at the nurse's station. Tommy kept on pacing. "I'm Catherine Lewis's pastor. Is this a good time for me to have a prayer with her?"

"It should be. Let's walk down there and see."

\* \* \*

Catherine sat propped up in her bed reading *Care of the Soul* by Thomas Moore. Suzanne recognized it. In fact it was on her desk to be read.

"Catherine, how are you?"

"Pastor, did you come all the way back from home just because of me?"

"I would have, but actually I haven't gone home yet. The children and I stay all day on Sunday and go home after their fellowship meeting. I usually make calls on Sundays, but I didn't expect to see you here today."

"I didn't either. They say I've had a stroke, but I feel fine."

"Your husband's out in the hall."

"I know. He was making me nervous so the nurses told him to give me a break."

"I see. You look relaxed. Is there anything you need, anyone you'd like me to call?"

"Would you pray? I can't seem to find any words."

"I'd be happy to. Prayers for healing?"

"Yes, healing or a quick death. And prayers for Mary, prayers for The Colonel. Mary's been with me ever since I was a young girl. She came with me from Virginia when I married. When my day comes, it will be difficult for both of them to know how to go on without me needing them so much. For the past twelve years they have spent most of their time taking care of me."

Suzanne sat down on the side of her bed and took her hand. "Let's pray. God of all creation, you have loved us even more than we love ourselves. We thank you for constant care all our lives. We come to you in this time of uncertainty. Catherine is unsure what is coming next. It's a time of change, which she hears blowing in the wind. She needs the comfort of your presence. We pray you will give her ways of being aware of you by her side.

"We ask for her healing and open ourselves to it coming in any ways possible: by means of the doctors, nurses, and others in this hospital; by her body's self-healing properties; by your Holy Spirit.

"We pray for Mary and Tommy that they will feel your presence with them today and always so that they know your peace and comfort. We, too, need that great gift of peace this day, tomorrow and all the tomorrows after that, even into eternity.

"In Jesus' name we pray. Amen"

Catherine wiped tears from her eyes and was thanking Suzanne when Tommy burst into the room.

"Why wouldn't they let me in? Are you okay?" He pushed Suzanne aside and took Catherine's hand. Suzanne left quietly.

# Chapter 13

THE next day, a few minutes after Suzanne sat down to make her list for the week, she heard Mildred.

"Yoohoo," she called and came through Liz's office. "Where's Liz?"

"Getting the mail. What's up, Mildred?"

"Well, I'm glad she isn't here," she whispered. "I wanted to mention something to you. Has she been using the coffee pot in the parlor kitchen?"

"We both do, why?"

"Well," she said with a wave of her hand as she tiptoed over to the table and sat down, "that coffee pot belongs to the Women's Association, and they won't like it if you use it."

"Really? That surprises me. I assumed it belonged to the church. We buy our own coffee, you know."

She raised her hands and gave a helpless shrug. "Also, I understand the children have been playing the grand piano in the parlor."

"And?"

"Well." She leaned forward. "The Colonel gave that piano to the church, and he doesn't like for people to play it."

"Hmmm," Suzanne said. "Has he complained to you about who's playing it?"

"No, I haven't told him about it yet."

"Have any of the women complained about us using the coffee pot?"

"No, I just tell you these things so you can avoid any problems."

"I see. Mildred, I do need your help with things like this. If people come to you with a complaint, will you ask them to come to me? Tell them how easy it is to talk with me and solve problems."

"They won't do that. People depend on me to do the hard thing."

"Here's the second thing I'd like your help on. If they want you to do it for them, tell them you won't do that, but you will come with them if they want you to."

"Isn't that a lot harder? People don't want to complain directly."

"I know it seems easier to get someone else to do it for them, and in the short run maybe it is, but in the long run it doesn't help. I need to talk directly to people, get to know them and their concerns. You will be doing me a big favor if you will help with this."

"Sure, sure, I just want everything to run smoothly. Would you write down for me what I should say?"

"Of course. Thank you, Mildred. This will be very important, and I appreciate your help."

As soon as she left, whistling and two stepping on her way out, Suzanne drove to the hospital thinking, Mildred must not know about Catherine or she would have told me.

* * *

When Suzanne started down the hall, she saw a nurse leave Catherine's room and pull the door shut. Suzanne knocked softly and went in. Tommy was sitting in a chair by Catherine's bed, one hand holding hers, the other covering his face. His shoulders shook and she heard a sob. Suzanne tentatively placed a hand on his shoulder, and he jerked his head up.

His eyes were wide and wild. She took another look at Catherine.

Her face was peaceful, but white and still. She wasn't sleeping. No, it can't be. Just yesterday she talked, she read, we prayed.

She looked back at Tommy. He still held onto his wife with one hand and sobbed into his other one. Suzanne didn't know what to say. That huge and powerful man sat broken in front of her. She looked for tissues and finally went to the nurses' station to get some. Back in the room, she put the box where he could reach it. Finally, she whispered, "I'm so sorry."

"So sudden. She smiled and then—." His voice broke. "All those machines and doctors and nurses. They should have been able to get her back. But she's gone and... she's gone."

"This is a terrible shock," she said. "I'm sure many of your friends and family will feel that, too, though not as strongly as you do. But we will walk this road with you. One day at a time, one minute at a time."

JJ walked in and Suzanne moved out of the way.

He knelt down beside Tommy. "Colonel, I'm here."

Tommy nodded his head.

"You let me know when you're ready," JJ said. "Take your time, as much time as you want. I'll be right outside the door."

Suzanne walked out with him. "You do that well," she said.

"What?"

"You let him know you were here to take Catherine when he's ready, and yet you were nearly invisible. Your presence didn't seem to interrupt his thoughts."

"I never thought about it," JJ said. "I just do it the way my dad did."

"I think it's that you didn't need anything from him emotionally."

He nodded. "I'm glad that's how it comes across. You know, she's been sick for a long time. But it's still unexpected. No matter how many times I go through this with people, my heart breaks for them. I think it's because their love can't be recovered or replaced."

"Yes, I've thought similarly," Suzanne said. "It's the end of all hopes for the relationship, too. I wonder how Tommy will handle this."

# CHAPTER 14

TOMMY paced around the funeral home's conference table and didn't look up when Suzanne entered the room with JJ. John and Bronwen sat at the table, looking at pictures of coffins. Mary stood against the wall as though waiting for her master's orders. She always acts like that, Suzanne thought. I wonder if it's a hold over from slave and servant days or if Tommy insisted on it. Or it could be what Catherine expected.

JJ handed Suzanne a folder and left. She shook hands with each one. "I'm sorry for your loss. Such a shock. Lovely lady." She cleared her throat and sat down.

"JJ says you want to celebrate Catherine's life day after tomorrow. Is it too soon for you to talk about that? We can plan the service now, or if you prefer I will come by your house later."

She looked at Tommy who murmured, "Let's do it now." He sat down and rested his forehead in his hands. Suzanne tried to relax, but Tommy's unpredictability made her self-conscious. Anything she said might unleash his rage.

She took a deep breath and motioned to Mary. "Come have a seat at the table, Mary. I see from what JJ gave me that you want the service at 10 AM at the church with burial afterward in the Welsh Cove Cemetery. In the Service of the Resurrection, we worship God and as part of that worship we will thank God for Catherine's life. Let's do our best to honor and celebrate her life. I've known her a very short time so I need your help. Is there anything particular you want included?"

They looked thoughtful but were silent. Suzanne glanced through the folder. "Here's a list of scripture verses Catherine wanted us to use."

"Is Psalm 23 on there? I always find that comforting," John said.

Bronwen added, "And the part in John 14 about 'in my Father's house are many mansions.' That means a lot to me."

"She listed those two and some others and also hymns: 'Be Thou My Vision,' 'I Need Thee Every Hour,' 'All Through the Night,' 'Crug Y Bar.' I don't know that last one."

"It's a burial song," Bronwen said. "The choir will sing it in Welsh."

"What about 'Suddenly There's a Valley?'" Suzanne asked. "It's not here."

"No," Tommy said. There was an awkward silence.

His brother John asked, "Are you sure, Tommy? You don't have to sing it. Robert could."

"No. Catherine hated that song."

"Hated it?" Bronwen asked. "It's the only thing I remember from Rose's service? Catherine and I both asked you to sing it then."

"I tell you she hated that song. It's not true."

"The song?" Bronwen asked.

Tommy stood up at his full and intimidating height and yelled, "The song is not true."

They all stared at him and held their collective breath.

Finally Suzanne said, "Okay, if you don't want it, that's settled. Now, tell me more about Catherine."

John began with details of her moving with Tommy from Virginia after the war and her delight in decorating their house.

"She planned all the gardens," Bronwen said.

Tommy coughed and finally managed in a choked voice to say, "She liked those bushes that look like deer."

"How long have you been married?" Suzanne asked.

He didn't answer. She looked at him hard, but he had his hands in front of his face, and his shoulders shook. She didn't press him.

"Fifty-eight years," Mary whispered then went on tentatively, glancing from time to time at Tommy. "She was always kind to me, a real lady."

"You came with her from Virginia when she married?" Suzanne prompted.

"Yes, she's the best friend I ever had, even before we came here. And she always treated me like a friend, not a... a..." Her voice faded off.

"Let's get this over with," Tommy said. "The choir will sing and everybody will sing hymns. All the usual ones. And include whatever is in her notes and her Bible." He pulled a small Bible from his coat pocket and slid it across the table to Suzanne. The white had greyed, the edges were worn and it was full of bookmarks and little papers expanding it to twice its original thickness.

\* \* \*

Back in the office, Suzanne made an outline, filling it in with what she had learned from the conversation with the family and in the information JJ had given her. She stopped when she read one of the scripture readings Catherine had listed for her service, Revelation 17:1.

"And there came one of the seven angels, which had the seven vials, and talked with me, saying unto me, Come hither; I will shew unto thee the judgment of the great whore that sitteth upon many waters."

The great whore? Suzanne stopped, checked the reference again and reread it. Why would she want this read? What does it have to do with death? Maybe it's because it's about judgment at the end. No, it doesn't make sense. More likely the chapter and verses have been written down wrong.

She called JJ. "I'm reading Catherine's file, and one of the scriptures she chose doesn't really fit. I'm wondering if it was typed wrong. Do you have an original, perhaps in her handwriting?"

"Let me check," JJ said. She heard him opening and shutting drawers. Finally, he came back. "Okay, I have her list. Which one is it?"

"Revelation 17:1."

"Yep, that's what I've got."

"Hmmm. It's about the great whore. I'm looking in the King James Version, assuming that would be what she would read."

"Don't you have her Bible there?"

"Oh, yes. It's in my briefcase. Let me check. Yes, it's King James all right. Maybe she transposed the numbers."

"Look in her Bible. She may have underlined a verse with similar numbers."

"Okay, let's see here. JJ, I don't know what to do with this. She has those verses underlined. And she specifically asked to have it included. But I'm not comfortable doing that. Let's see if she got the numbers mixed up. Maybe it was Revelation 1:17. Thank God, it's underlined, too. It's familiar. 'Fear not, I am the first and the last.' Okay, that fits. Surely she meant that one."

JJ chuckled. "You would cause a major scandal in Middletown if you mentioned 'The Great Whore' at Catherine's funeral. Hey, I've got a question for you about the Bible. Are you walking to lunch today?"

"Yes, shall I stop by?"

"Sure, let's go see what Pete has cooking. I'll treat since I'm going to make you work."

JJ had begun reading the suggested Bible readings for Sundays, the ones she usually preached from. His questions and observations often gave her a way to approach the message, and every now and then he'd come up with a story or illustration that fit.

"I've been wondering," he said as they walked, "how you respond when people ask about the verse that says women shouldn't speak in church?"

She could answer that question in her sleep. "Do you want the five minute or two hour answer?" she said.

JJ held up five fingers.

"That's from Paul. He gave specific instructions to individual churches concerning whatever was going with them. If they had trouble with noisy women interfering with worship, he told them to sit down and be quiet. And so forth. He also wrote that slaves should obey their masters. But then in the letter to the church at Galatia, he says, 'There is neither Jew nor Greek, there is neither slave nor free, there is neither male or female; for you are all one in Christ Jesus.' Paul emphasized grace and the law of love not the law of rules. His bottom line was always how to truly worship God and follow Jesus.'"

JJ grinned, "You have that memorized."

"Oh, yes."

"Well, then when you're reading the Bible, how do you know whether it is directed to you or if it's for someone else?"

"Look to Jesus. Read the scriptures through him. He said not to take away from any of the laws but to understand them and see them all as ways to express of love for God above all else and love for your neighbor as you love yourself. I think of it as going deeper than the rules, deeper in love. If a rule is against love, it isn't of God."

"Do other people believe that way?" he asked as they sat down at the corner table by the window.

"I've found that people usually do when they read the Bible as a whole and see its progression. Then they see the unfolding revelation by God. They also see how God's people developed over the years in their understanding of God."

"Where do you suggest I start?" he asked. "See, I want to know... um, how do I put this? I want understand it better."

"Is there anything particular you're searching for?"

"No, it's just that I want to know if what I'm reading applies to me."

"I suggest you start by reading Luke and see if you have any questions about what's in that gospel."

\* \* \*

Back in her office Suzanne wondered if she had answered his question. I'm not sure I understood what he was asking, she thought. I'm too tired. Maybe sometime when I haven't had to deal with Tommy and death and funeral planning, I'll be able to communicate better.

# CHAPTER 15

SUZANNE left the office early that afternoon. "Liz, I'm going home. If anyone calls or comes by, I'll call them tomorrow afternoon. I'm going to stay home in the morning and prepare the funeral service."

She felt weepy all the way home, and instead of taking the cut off to go home the back way, she went on into town to Bell's office.

He stood in his secretary's office examining some papers with her, but looked up when Suzanne entered the doorway. He waved her into his office.

"What's up?" He took her coat, handed her a cup of coffee and sat down at his desk. She took both his cup and hers to set them on his desk, and then moved to sit on his lap.

He sat still, no hug, no response as she leaned in and kissed him. She sat back and looked him in the eye. "What?"

"I'm not comfortable with this in the office."

"Hmmm." She moved to the table and blinked back tears.

"I'm surprised to see you in the middle of the day. Is anything wrong?"

"Just need a hug."

"I know you had a rough day Sunday with the tornado scare. We haven't had a chance to talk, but Peter and Julie filled me in on the way to school yesterday. Anything else going on?"

"The tornado was just the beginning. We made it to church barely

97

in time for worship and then Sadie Ross was there and stayed after church and we had lunch and talked. And then Tommy's wife Catherine was taken to the hospital so I went over there." She paused and caught her breath. "Catherine, Tommy's wife, died yesterday. I met with the family today, funeral Thursday." Suzanne tried to keep her voice strong and even. She didn't want pity. She didn't want him to say, "I told you so" about taking that position at Covenant Church. But she was running on empty and needed something.

He joined her at the table. "What can I do for you?"

Now the tears flowed, and she couldn't stop them. An occasional sob and hiccup betrayed her. "What's happened to us?"

"What do you mean?"

"I feel so far away from you. Is it because I took this job? Are you angry?"

"I don't know what you're talking about. We're coordinating our schedules to take care of everything, aren't we?"

"I mean you and me. We don't spend time together. Even when we're in the same room, I don't feel like you're there. All we do is talk about the kids and the house or our schedules and plans."

"Hey, we're going to Alabama, aren't we? Just get through Advent and Christmas Eve. We can leave after the midnight service and drive through the night, or if you prefer, we can get up real early Christmas morning. If you want to, we can stop half way and make the trip in two days. Of course, if we do that both ways, we'll only be there for three days and it would be expensive."

"Oh, I don't care," she said wiping her eyes.

"Hey, let's go take a walk. I need to go to the post office and sign for a letter. There was a notice in our mailbox at home."

Suzanne put on her coat without thinking. She had no energy to make decisions.

At the post office, Bell signed for the thick envelope. "It's from your mother," he said. "What do you think it is?" He handed the envelope to Suzanne.

Outside, at the top of the long flight of steps to the street, she sat down on a bench and opened it. "It's tickets, plane tickets for us to fly on Christmas Day and back on Thursday, New Year's Eve. We can have all week there. How thoughtful of her. We won't be so tired when we get back."

"I don't know if I can stay that long," Bell said.

"What do you mean? We planned to get back on Thursday anyway."

"It just seems too long to be away."

"Bell, I think we need to see a counselor."

He stared at her, eyes narrowed and lips tight. "I don't feel the need for that." He steered her out of the post office.

"I do. Will you go with me?"

"Can't you work this out on your own? It'll be all over town if we go see anyone. That could ruin my effectiveness. Tell me what's bothering you and we'll figure it out."

"We haven't made love in months. I'm worried about you drinking so much beer. You don't seem to care about what I'm feeling. And I'm not feeling loved."

He shook his head. "Where does all this come from? Out of the blue, in the middle of the holidays, you lay all this on me?"

"I don't want to be a nag so I don't bring up things all the time, but surely you remember that I have mentioned how much beer you're drinking and how we need to have a date night every now and then."

"You have to do more than drop hints if you're really concerned about something."

They walked back to the church in silence. When they reached her car, he said, "I have to get to a meeting with the mayor. We're planning a citywide 'Help Your Neighbor' campaign and she's going to be in all our publicity. There's so much going on between now and Christmas, I can't think about anything but getting through the holiday. Let's wait until we get back from Alabama to talk about all this. Go on home and take a long hot bath. I'll take care of dinner tonight."

She shrugged her shoulders. Maybe I'm just tired and everything feels worse than it is.

\* \* \*

As soon as Suzanne walked in the door, the phone rang. "Suzanne, it's Bertha."

"Bertha, I haven't talked to you for weeks. How are you and how are things at Harvest Church?"

"I'm fine, but we've had a death and I knew you'd want to know. Minnie passed away in the night."

"Minnie? Had she been sick?" she asked, thinking, I should have gone out to see the folks at Harvest before now.

"No. She has been fine. Died in her sleep, the way she always said she wanted to go. I went over there when she didn't answer the phone. She looked peaceful. The twins want you to do the funeral."

"Bertha, I have to be careful not to step on your new pastor's toes. They should ask him."

"I know. I told them that, but the thing is our new pastor left yesterday to go see his parents in California. He left it up to me to take care of anything like this. So I think it would be okay, more than okay. It would be just what Minnie would want. And her sons."

"I see. It would be good to see all of you. Peter asked me yesterday when we could go to Harvest again. We all hate that we have to be at a school concert the night of the chicken noodle supper. So, tell me when do they want the funeral?"

"Thursday at 10."

"Oh, no, I already have a funeral on Thursday at ten."

"Just a minute."

Suzanne heard her talking to someone.

"Danny Canny is here and says, as far as the funeral home is concerned, we can move it to Friday morning."

"Will her sons be okay with that?"

"Yes, they said to make whatever arrangements we could and they'd be happy with them."

"Harvest Church won't be the same without her."

"No," Bertha said. "One by one we're going to be saying goodbye and going home, you know. We're all of that age."

"Hmmm," Suzanne said and caught herself. There's that 'hmmm' Bell doesn't like. "Bertha, I don't know how I'm going to find a time to meet with Richard and Robert about the service."

"I'll call you when I know they are arriving. Or maybe they will call you to talk."

"Okay. But I'll be busy all Thursday with this other funeral."

"I'll let you know. Tell me, how are things going? Last time we talked you were still trying to find what keeps that congregation in conflict."

"Not much progress on isolating the main problem. But I'm getting to know some of the dynamics involved."

"You once told me that the first thing to do is learn to love them."

"Yes, but Bell thinks I need to claim my authority and man up."

"Well, I don't know about that, but I do know you have great gifts for persistent love and wisdom."

"Bertha, you are the wise woman and such a good friend to me. I couldn't have made it through my time at Harvest without you."

Suzanne hung up and felt her mind float and her emotions sink until she was not connected with either one. She got a bowl of ice cream and a crossword puzzle and took them to the bathtub where she soaked and let her mind wander. The funeral for Catherine probably needs to be rather formal, the one for Minnie—dear Minnie, gone. How shall we talk about her life as we celebrate it? She was so, so unique. This will be hard on her sons. And Catherine leaves Tommy all alone. I wonder if he will become even more angry and bitter about life. What can I say in these funerals that will bring the gospel to their situations?

She wrapped up in a soft robe and climbed into bed, snuggling down and trying to turn her mind off. The phone rang. Her whole body tensed as though about to receive a blow. Please, God, no more death, no more emergencies right now.

"Suzanne, it's JJ. Nobody died. People always think I'm calling with bad news. I just wondered if you're okay. You seemed a little down at lunch."

"JJ, you're a good friend. I thought I covered it well, but, yes, I am a little down."

"On overload?"

"Yes. And another funeral to do Friday at my last church. Their pastor is out of town."

"You've taken on a lot with this church. What can I do to help?"

"Oh, talking with you always lifts me up. I guess I'll take a nap. Maybe some rest will help."

"Okay. Here's the latest joke for you. This couple went out on a blind date, and within the first fifteen minutes she said, 'I don't believe in one night stands.' Her date agreed. 'I don't either. Every bedroom needs two nightstands and two lamps.'"

Suzanne laughed in spite of herself.

"Hey, will you call me if you need to talk?"

"I sure will, JJ. Thanks. Thanks a lot for calling." She fell asleep feeling warm and cared for. He was just what she needed.

The next morning she called Liz and asked if she had any messages? "No" was the right answer. She stayed in bed all day with her books and note pad at hand and outlined the rest of the week:

funeral Thursday, funeral Friday, sermon Sunday. Then she finished writing Catherine's service and started on Minnie's.

It would be impossible to capture Minnie's life and do it justice. She grew up in California but moved to Kansas when her husband retired from the Navy. They lived in the home where he had grown up, but their sons, grown by the time they moved back, had stayed in California and established a chain of shoe stores, which catered to the rich and famous.

The twins, Richard and Robert matched Minnie's mischievousness. One never knew what to expect.

Bertha called. "There won't be time to visit with Minnie's sons before the service, but each of them will offer some thoughts when we celebrate their mother's life."

Lord, help us, Suzanne thought.

# CHAPTER 16

JJ picked up Suzanne at the church, with Catherine in the "wagon," a beautiful black Cadillac hearse. "The old folks still call it 'the wagon' even though they haven't actually used one in years," he said. "A Welsh funeral is a little different, lots of tradition that may not be familiar to you." They drove to Tommy's. "Notice all the curtains in his house are drawn tight. They will be opened after the burial."

In front of the house about twenty people, bundled up like carolers, sang, "Bread of Heaven, bread of heaven, feed me till I want no more. Feed me till I want no more."

"Come with me to the door," JJ said. "We'll escort Tommy to the wagon and the singers will drive ahead of us to the church."

\* \* \*

When Jewell Edwards had gone over the music for the service with Suzanne, she said, "We'll sing a little slower than usual. And be forewarned. All these songs are tear jerkers. We Welsh have two kinds of music, sad and sadder. Tommy asked Robert to sing, 'Abide With Me' at the cemetery. That always chokes me up."

Suzanne usually included both sadness of loss and joy of the resurrection in a service, including stories or memories that brought both tears and smiles, but she stayed on the somber side, taking her cue from JJ's description and Jewell's music.

Flowers covered the front of the sanctuary. One standing arrange-
ment of chrysanthemums displayed the Welsh flag, a green and white
background with a red dragon in the center. A blanket of white roses
covered the casket.

Suzanne focused the service on the resurrection and the scripture
from John 14 in which Jesus assured his disciples that he was going
to prepare a place for them and that he would come again and take
them there. From her conversations with them, it seemed to Suzanne
that Tommy and his sister-in-law Bronwen needed reassurance about
eternal life. However, she knew that in the midst of grief her words
might not be heard. From the front pew, where he sat with John,
Bronwen and Mary, Tommy stared at the floor throughout the whole
service.

Sniffs, an occasional sob, and one loud blowing of the nose sprin-
kled throughout the service kept the focus on sadness, even though
Suzanne emphasized the resurrection promise.

At the cemetery the sun shone, but without warmth. And no trees
broke the chill of the prairie wind. Robert's hair blew back and forth
as he sang a plaintive last verse of "Abide With Me." As she predicted,
Jewell's tears flowed freely as her son sang.

> *Hold thou thy cross before my closing eyes;*
> *Shine through the gloom and point me to the skies.*
> *Heaven's morning breaks and earth's vain shadows flee;*
> *In life, in death, O Lord, abide with me.*

Afterward, tea was served at the church. A long table covered
with lacy cloth held a silver tea service at one end and coffee at
the other with mints, breads and little crustless sandwiches in the
middle. Mildred served tea, her back rigid and legs properly crossed
at the ankles. At the other end of the table, a woman Suzanne didn't

know sat in the same posture, pouring coffee from a silver pot into delicate china cups.

Tommy moved from table to table shaking hands. When he came to Suzanne, he simply put a hand on her shoulder while talking to other people.

* * *

Suzanne started Minnie's service the same as Catherine's. "We are gathered here to worship God and in that worship to celebrate the life of Minnie, her life completed now in its purposes. Today we share the loss we feel and we share what will go on living of her life, for she is a part of each of us."

Worshipers filled the little church, which sat in the middle of wheat fields. The beautiful painting of Jesus and the Lambs looked out over the pews. When it came time to share stories of Minnie's life, many spoke. Robert and Richard finished the recollections by telling about her brush with acting in movies. They each wore one of her dramatic shawls. To outsiders the laughter would have appeared sacrilegious and disrespectful. But Suzanne knew of the close bonds they had and the love with which they celebrated her life and her eccentricities.

At the end of the service they surprised Suzanne by pulling out a trumpet and a trombone from the choir stall and playing their mother out of the church with "When the Saints Go Marching In." She would have loved it, Suzanne thought. She would have loved it, and I hope somehow she knows.

The cemetery was like the one Catherine was buried in, stark and lonely, open to the chilly wind except for a useless tent. Everyone came to endure the moment. Suzanne ended with, "We celebrate Minnie's life and all that will go on living of her life. But we will miss her body, her physical presence. It housed her spirit. And although her body does not house her spirit any more, it is how we knew her.

Let us in this time acknowledge that we commit her body and her spirit to God's care, her soul to God's mercy. We offer her back into God's arms."

After the solemn "Amen" from the congregation, Suzanne shook hands with the family sitting in a row of chairs. Then Robert and Richard stood up with their horns and played "Nearer my God to Thee." One by one the mourners gradually joined in until they all sang together, "Still all my song shall be, nearer my God to thee; nearer my God to thee, nearer to thee!"

Suzanne found it difficult to leave the cemetery—so cold, so windy, leaving Minnie as they had left Catherine, all alone.

\* \* \*

Back at Harvest church a meal awaited them, ham and beans, corn-bread, gelatin salad. And Robert and Richard brought in a five-tiered wedding cake.

Bertha repeated Suzanne's thoughts, "Minnie would have loved this."

# CHAPTER 17

SUZANNE stood in a hole cut out of the center of a round communion table. Flat boards two feet wide circled the opening. They formed four concentric circles, and each ring was covered in spiral designs. The most central board stayed in place and held a chalice and plate of bread. The other three moved independently of each other. They held a merry-go-round of animals which moved around and around, up and down, each one ridden by a costumed person wearing a mask. They sped up and slowed down with no particular rhythm or coordination with each other or the organ music which crescendoed and then suddenly diminished to sweetness. The second ring started moving backwards. Some riders laughed heartily, some sobbed. Suzanne grew dizzier and dizzier until she fell down and was swept under the table.

* * *

When she awoke Saturday morning, Suzanne stayed in bed and wrote down what she could remember of the dream. Then she set it aside to begin making notes for the next day's sermon. However, her mind wouldn't work. I should have said no to the second funeral, she thought. I'm too tired. But how could I have refused Minnie's service?

* * *

The rest of December, Suzanne moved in a cloud. She wrote sermons, visited in the hospital, bought gifts, and planned Christmas Eve services, but her heart hovered somewhere behind her, never quite catching up.

On Christmas Eve, a light snow added joy to the candlelight services. And the next day the family flew to Huntsville, Alabama. Suzanne slept through the flight, not even waking at their stop in Dallas. When they arrived, Julie had to shake her awake.

Her whole family met them at the airport, her mother and father and all three sisters. Suzanne fell into their arms and wished they could carry her to the car.

She stayed in a daze through the gift giving and the familiar, comforting turkey dinner. Finally, she went to bed and slept twelve hours in a deep sleep, knowing her parents would take care of locking the doors, being sure the children were okay, turning out the lights, and all those other details she gladly shed when she was in their house.

Suzanne's parents lived in a neighborhood outside of Athens, Alabama. Their new brick ranch easily housed them, but home would always be her grandparents' house out in the country. Now, Suzanne's sister Elizabeth lived there with her husband and three children. It became the gathering place where the four sisters and their mother sat by the fireplace in the kitchen sharing much laughter, many pots of coffee, and the joys of their lives.

The children, twelve cousins in all, ran through the woods searching for arrowheads and remnants of the old hotel which had stood on the land in the 1800's. Julie brought back fossils and interesting rocks to show everyone and packed them away to take home. Bell spent hours with Suzanne's dad in his workshop. They always had a project, this time making bookends.

One morning Suzanne suggested to Bell that they take a hike through the woods. He was right, she thought. I was tired that day

110

I suggested going to a counselor. But sometimes being tired prompts a person to say what has been hiding deep within. I could go on as everyone expects me to, but while both of us are rested, I'm going to find just the right words to geet him to understand. Sadie had given her the name of a counselor in Topeka at Menninger's. If he won't go, she thought, I'll go by myself as soon as I get the time. But the children ran through the woods yelling like a bear was after them. And when they caught up to Suzanne and Bell, they chattered away. She never found the right time.

Suzanne cried when they got on the plane to go home. She hugged her sister Melanie goodbye. "I don't know why I live so far from the people I love." She missed them already and didn't want to leave the comfort of being herself instead of a person whose roles as pastor and mother—though she loved being both—hid her real self. Now she would go back and fall into those roles again.

On the plane she remembered Sadie's words, "Don't expect the honeymoon to last. Pastors come and pastors go for a congregation. They aren't your family even though it feels like it sometimes."

This is my family, she thought. I should give more of myself to them. In the new year I'm going to call them more often.

# 1988

## CHAPTER 18

"**M**OM, what do you think about fags?"

Suzanne stopped and stared at Peter. They stood on the familiar sidewalk between the church and Pete's Diner. It was the first Sunday of the new year. Sarah's mother had taken the girls to a movie and Matthew had stayed home sick with a cold so Suzanne and Peter had a rare Sunday afternoon together.

"You should see your face?" Peter laughed.

"That's not a nice word. Where did you hear it?"

"Some kids at school called me that, and then I heard some boys here say that about somebody else."

"It's an offensive word for "gay" or "homosexual.""

"Grandad called them that when he got angry at Christmas."

She nodded. At one meal her dad had ranted on and on about her cousin Sam. "Don't even mention his name in this house. Disgraceful. He's gone off to California and doesn't even keep in touch with his mother. Kids wouldn't get such ideas in their heads if people would stop talking about it."

Her sister Melanie bravely spoke up. "Dad, I have students who have obviously been uncomfortable with their sexuality since they were young children. I think they were born that way. People are just now becoming aware of how prevalent homosexuality is. One of these days, there will be understanding and acceptance."

"Never! It's not natural. Besides..." He raved on and on, until he made himself so upset he left the table.

Peter brought her back to the moment. "Do you know that man waving at us?"

"JJ, hello. Are you coming back from Pete's?" she asked.

"Yep, sure am. Be sure to try their carrot cake. Who's this, the famous Peter Hawkins?"

Suzanne introduced them. "Peter, JJ. I pointed out his house back a few blocks. He's become a really good friend to me."

"Your mother is a breath of fresh air in Middletown. What grade are you in?"

Peter and JJ chatted for a few moments about Christmas in Alabama, and then they all moved on. Peter was not distracted from his questions.

"So, what do you think?" he asked.

Suzanne took a deep breath. "Nobody ever mentioned homosexuality when I was growing up, and I didn't know what it meant until I was in college. Let me just talk a while and see if I can make sense of it.

"As I understand it, boys and girls may have crushes on a teacher or a coach or someone their own sex in junior high or early high school, and that's not homosexuality. It's a part of growing up and seeing who you want to be like. But sometimes a boy gets a little older and not only wants to be with boys to do sports and hang out, but also wants to hug and kiss and things like that. And he isn't interested in doing that with girls. Then it takes a lot of thinking and figuring out if that is the way his life will be. It is a difficult life. My cousin Sam went to California because his parents were embarrassed by him. His dad gave him a hard time, told him he walked like a girl and made fun of him."

114

"That's really sad."

They reached Pete's and stood outside talking. "It sure is," Suzanne said, "and I can't believe that kind of rejection is right. Someone like Sam needs our compassion not our anger. I hope you'll never call a gay person names. I think the closest I can come to understanding this is to imagine what it would feel like to be attracted to a woman and want to marry her and live together forever. I can't imagine it. Maybe it's as hard for Sam to know what it's like to be the way I am."

"Why do people get so angry about it?"

"That's a good question. I think maybe they're afraid."

"Afraid of what?"

"I'm not sure. Do you have any ideas?"

"No."

"Peter, has anyone made you uncomfortable, like expecting something physically?"

"Mom! No, nothing like that."

"Okay, I had to ask. It would be a hard life for you. I'd love you anyway, but I think you're a little young to know."

"Mom! Stop it. I know I'm not. I just want to know what to say when people say things about someone else."

"All right. Let's go on in and talk about that over lunch."

# CHAPTER 19

NINE elders and five youth choir members sat around the table in the church library.

"We'd only use the fellowship hall," Robert said. "My parents said they would help supervise, and we'll be sure there is no damage. It's just tutoring."

"Those people don't know how to take care of things," Bronwen said. "And they'd probably be running all over the building."

There was a long silence. Then Morgan, the youngest elder, spoke up. "We have asked every group in the church to consider doing something for others—at least one project a year. The youth choir has considered several possibilities, but this is the one they decided on. They know kids at school who have come from Vietnam, Thailand and Mexico. Did you know the meat processing plant recruits them and brings them here? Those of us who teach know that most of these kids and their parents are not only illiterate in English, they are also illiterate in their native language. They can't read or write at all. I think it is a wonderful idea to help them learn to read English. I'll help with this, and surely others will have compassion for this project, too."

"Who's going to clean up after them?" Bronwen asked.

"I will." Peter raised his hand.

Bronwen sat with her arms folded and her lips pressed tightly together. Her husband John looked at Suzanne and took a breath. "John, you have something to add?"

He nodded and said, "I'll help."

Morgan sat up straight. "Good. You know we went to Vietnam and bombed their country to kingdom come. We owe them some help."

Two of the older men looked down at the table and frowned.

Suzanne opened her mouth to call for the vote when Bronwen raised her hand. "I move to table the motion until the next meeting."

"A move to table is not debatable. We vote a simple up or down, majority rules," Suzanne said.

"The motion to table until the next meeting passes five to four," Suzanne announced. "Young people, we will be discussing this at our next meeting. It will give us some time to consider all the implications. Thank you for bringing this idea here. We commend you on your sensitivity to the needs of others in our community, and we will let you know if this particular way to help them will fit with the plans and concerns of the whole church."

The youth choir left, looking at each other, and whispering. Peter stormed out, scowling and clenching his fists.

Morgan's fiery eyes and raised hand showed Suzanne this was not over. "Since this is tabled until the next meeting, I move we meet on Sunday after church so that we can report back to the young people before their next rehearsal."

"I second that," John said. Bronwen gave him a quick frown.

The motion passed. "I'll order pizza and we can meet right after church," Suzanne said. "As you are thinking about this before then, let's use it as an exercise to learn the levels of conflict. This is a relatively easy difference of opinion that we have, but if we practice on it, we can learn how to keep things like this at the level of a problem to solve instead of letting disagreements escalate to the point that we can't resolve them.

"If there is no objection, I will give you the short version of Levels of Conflict so we can apply them in this situation." Silence reigned.

Suzanne flipped the newsprint to a clean page and wrote near the bottom, Level 0. On the line above that she wrote Level 1. "Level 0 is avoidance of all conflict. You may find that after going through a disturbing or anxious time, you will avoid disagreeing or stating your opinion on matters. That is a natural reaction to try to keep everything on an even keel. This is not healthy because the concerns and differences go underground and can't be dealt with together. They tend to blow up later, bigger and worse, destroying relationships.

"Level 1 is a problem to solve. This is where we are right now as we consider the tutoring program the young people have proposed. If we can keep ourselves at Level 1, we can treat this as a problem we want to solve together. We'll state our different opinions, as we have tonight, respecting each other. And we'll work cooperatively to sort it out.

"However, if what we want becomes more important than solving the problem, we'll begin to feel angry with whoever stands in the way of what we want. Then we escalate to Level 2, taking the matter personally.

"If the conflict progresses we will take sides, talk about 'us' and 'them.' We may hear ourselves say the words, 'they always' or 'they never.' At that level we have begun to affect our unity. You see how at the level of a problem to solve, we haven't been accusing anyone or questioning motives. However, as we move to higher levels we do that and may even escalate to "This church isn't big enough for both of us." Beyond that we hear people say, "That person doesn't deserve to be a church member or a minister." And at the highest level, "That person doesn't deserve to be alive."

Suzanne filled in the levels one to five and hesitated, wondering, Is that clear? Do I need to say more?

John was watching her intently and taking notes. "Would you bring that newsprint on Sunday?"

"Sure."

Morgan chimed in, "So, we need to keep this proposal of tutoring students as a problem to solve together."

"Right."

The others looked thoughtful. Even Bronwen made some notes and asked for clarification.

"Do you see how this might help us with more difficult subjects?" Suzanne asked.

"Like what?" Morgan said.

"Like allowing queers in the church," Otto said. His double chins wobbled and his white hair trembled with angry tension. He hardly ever spoke. Heads jerked up.

"Let's use the correct word and speak kindly," Suzanne said.

Otto's friend Hugh spoke up. "Yeah, that's a problem to solve all right. There's not a one of those people in this church, whatever you call them, and I hope to never see it. You let one in and pretty soon you'll have those, those whatever you call them, holding hands and kissing in the pews."

"Order, order, please. Be recognized if you want to speak."

Suzanne finally got them quieted down, but even after she called for quiet, Hugh said, "Some people even want ministers who are that way."

Otto chimed in, "It's not natural."

And Bronwen said, "We shouldn't be talking about this in the church."

"That's a hot button topic, for sure," Suzanne said. "Look how quickly we began feeling agitated and assuming people with an opinion different from ours are all wrong.

If we presented that for a topic tonight, how else might we begin the discussion?"

Morgan looked thoughtful and then hesitantly said, "You mean keeping it at a problem to solve?"

"Yes, how could we do that?"

Morgan said, "We could tell what we know. Like, I've read that one in every nine men is homosexual."

Anna said, "We could study, find out if that is true."

"We could state our views calmly and say, 'In my opinion,'" John said.

Morgan leaned forward across the table. "We could tell stories. Like, my friend Sharon's son is dying. He lives in California, has AIDS. Sharon told her best friend, and her friend won't talk to her any more. Just abandoned her, right when she needed support the most." Morgan was on a roll, talking faster and louder. "We could speak from our knowledge of Jesus and his love. For instance, I know you people. You wouldn't turn your back on my friend. Whether you believed her son was born that way or she brought him up to be gay or he made the choice to be. You are loving people. You wouldn't abandon her."

Suzanne finally stopped her. "Morgan, those are some good ways to proceed when that topic rises to the top of our agenda. Thank you." I should have stopped her from going on that long, discussing the issue. I hope no one calls me on it.

"Well, now, doesn't a tutoring program sound tame?" Suzanne said.

# CHAPTER 20

O NE Saturday Suzanne and Bell dropped Peter and Julie at the library and drove to the grocery store. "Bell, I've been meaning to tell you that Peter wants to know about homosexuality. I gather some kids at school called him names, and he didn't know what they meant."

"Oh, God, please don't tell me he thinks he's gay," Bell said. "He's much too young to know, and I don't think he could be. He isn't at all effeminate. That long hair and earring don't mean anything."

"He's not worried about that but wants to know what to say when someone calls a person names. We had a good talk over lunch yesterday. But I wondered if you covered everything with your 'birds and bees' talk."

"Well, I didn't talk about that!"

"Does he know about—?"

Bell interrupted, "I covered the basics. He's informed enough for his age. How is Covenant Church coming along? Have you found the source of their conflict?"

She wasn't fooled at all by him changing the subject. I'll have to be sure he did tell Peter enough, she thought.

"I've found too many sources for what's wrong at the church," she said. "They have a long history together which means their relationships are complex. I don't think any of them could say what the core problem is. I can see that the sexual misconduct of pastors has affected their ability to trust. And they are the result of three churches merging—you know how long that can be a difficulty. Then, too, one group of men used to control the money and how it was spent. That's when they had both trustees and elders in years past. So the Session would make decisions, but the trustees could stymie them by refusing to fund what they didn't like. Let's see, what else? Oh, one of the pastors they disagreed about died in the pulpit. It looks like every pastor became a football to be tossed around, one team for him and the other against. Then when a new pastor came, whoever favored the last one fought the new one.

"I know I can't unravel all this. I keep collecting information and observing carefully, hoping everything will become clear and I can see the whole picture. I'm on edge wondering what weirdness will pop up and slap me in the face. But I'm hoping if my relationship with them is clearcut, and we learn how to get along and solve problems together, we can bridge the gap between sides. If I can love them enough,..."

"Suzanne, you can't love everyone into behaving well."

# CHAPTER 21

Every three months Suzanne had to meet with the Committee on Ministry of the Presbytery, eighteen elected representatives of churches in Northern Kansas, half clergy, half elders. In their role of oversight for all the churches and their pastors, they required regular meetings with every interim pastor. She dreaded going. At her first meeting with them she received too much advice and had difficulty describing her style because she tended to watch and observe for a long time before prescribing anything. She knew that to some of them what she did sounded like doing nothing. They would probably echo Bell's words, "sounds like gobbledygook."

One man on the committee, Howard, had written "A Bible Study for Churches in Conflict" and insisted that it would solve all the problems in the world. He handed her a copy at that first meeting along with notes about how to use it.

Late in January on a Wednesday afternoon, she left Middletown and drove to Topeka to meet again with the committee at Saint Andrews Presbyterian, the home church of the moderator, Jan.

The meeting was in session when she arrived, and Suzanne hesitated at the door to the fellowship hall. The members sat around a large table made by pushing two together. Coffee cups, notebooks and scattered papers sat in front of them. She recognized several people. The Presbytery staff members, James Talley and Sadie Ross smiled at her.

Jan spotted her at the door. "Here she is. Come in, sit down. We'll move to the Order of the Day and pick up our discussion again afterward."

Several people got up to get coffee, and two men rearranged chairs at their corner of the table, pulling one up for her. Smiles, greetings and offers of coffee helped Suzanne feel welcome, as much as she could, while feeling like she was under a spotlight. She pulled her notes out, told her hands to stop shaking, and took a deep breath. You're not on trial, she told herself, even if it feels like it.

Jan called the meeting back to order. "You will remember that Rev. Hawkins went to serve as the interim pastor at Covenant Church in Middletown back in October. We met with her when she began her ministry there, and this is her three month check-in. Suzanne, we put you in a difficult situation there. Tell us where you are in the interim tasks and what it's been like for you."

"Thank you, Madam Moderator. Covenant Church is healthier than I expected in some ways and more confusing in others. These first months they have outdone themselves in welcoming my family and me. The first day I even received flowers from the Women's Association and chocolates from the elders currently on the Session." She paused for the expected "oohs." They didn't disappoint her.

"I find their financial situation and procedures to be quite solid with the exception of their pledges. One man supports 60% of the budget."

The men and women around the table hung on her every word. She saw two men whisper to each other and immediately thought, they're going to pick out something and challenge me.

"They have an administrative manual with descriptions of each committee's mission and duties. They have personnel policies which we've made minor tweaks to. So, organization and processes are in order. Before I leave, we will involve the whole congregation in envisioning what the future can be."

"Worship is quite wonderful. The music, the sanctuary—"

A man at the other end of the table broke in, "I hear the preaching isn't bad either." Laughter broke the tension and she smiled a silent thank you to him.

"I've tried to keep worship as a time of sanctuary for everyone and I've told them so. It's hard to know for sure, but I see some signs that we have accomplished that. There is a sense of peace on Sunday morning. Numbers are holding steady.

"Now, let's see." She consulted her notes. "Oh, yes. There is one man, the same one who contributes 60% of the budget, who hasn't appreciated the Presbytery's help in the past and still is angry about changes, specifically the unicameral leadership which did away with trustees. He also has a problem with a woman pastor. But when his wife died, he didn't object to me doing the funeral. He seems in general to be filled with anger and it comes out in rudeness and attempts to control everything and everyone around him.

"Programming is good. They have an especially good adult choir and youth choir. The youth fellowship group is thriving. Mission work consists mostly of financial aid to local charities although the youth have begun a tutoring program for children whose parents have been recruited from Vietnam, Thailand, and Mexico to work in the meat processing plant.

"Adult education is missing. We're planning to start a class."

"It seems to me that the main problem they have is in the area of relationships. On the surface they are polite and functioning well, but I hear of broken friendships, past hurts unhealed, and confusion. I'd say this is the area which needs the most attention."

Also, I've been teaching them the levels of conflict, and we've tried to keep minor disagreements at the level of a problem to solve, practicing in case a major conflict arises."

Suzanne paused and smiled. "That's the three minute summary."

"Thank you, Suzanne," Jan said. "Do you have any questions for Rev. Hawkins?"

"Yes, I do," Howard said. She knew what was coming. "Have you used 'The Bible Study for Churches in Conflict'?"

"I have read through it and will use it at the right time," she said. In truth she found it heavy handed with rules and thought it was likely to elicit resistance.

"Why haven't you used it?" he asked. "I'd have done that first thing."

"There are many good resources," she said. "I like to know what they are and be ready to use them at the most auspicious time."

A woman leaned around the man next to Suzanne and said, "It sounds to me like you have accomplished a great deal in three months. What do you plan to do next?"

"I will keep up with what I've already mentioned, but I think continuing to develop relationships is the most important task. And it's not just a task. It's a joy. There are wonderful, salt of the earth people in the Covenant Church. As we get to know each other better, I will note any difficulties and try to iron out problems in order to keep relationships healthy. I mean that in a natural and honest way, not a manipulative one. It was Sadie who first mentioned that the same dysfunction they've had with previous pastors will probably show up in their relationships with me. As we tend to difficulties and heal them, we will affect other relationships and the whole congregation."

One of the young pastors waved his hand at the moderator. "I've never heard of this before—the dysfunction showing up in their relationships with the pastor. Is that something the rest of you know about?"

Sadie spoke up. "It's a theory which is probably new to many of you. The thought is that the church is a system just as a body is a system. Each part affects the whole and the whole affects each part. If you change one part, you change the whole. If you heal one part of the church, it can affect the health of the whole church. I think that Pastor Suzanne will in some way experience what other pastors there have experienced, and the way she deals with it will affect that church. It's possible that she can be the catalyst for a new way of being."

An elder raised her hand, "As a goal, I can't see how it would be measurable, but —"

Howard interrupted her and held up a piece of paper. "That's not on the list of interim responsibilities."

The elder continued, "I was about to say that it sounds quite wise to me."

Sadie broke in. "Suzanne, you have accomplished a great deal of ground work in only three months. We are blessed to have you there. Are you taking care of yourself?"

That threw her. She hadn't prepared for anyone to ask about her well being. "Um, I guess so. Yes, I think I have. And my children go with me on Sundays. We spend the whole day there. We have lunch together and then they do homework and go to youth choir and fellowship, while I make calls or have meetings. It's actually working out very well."

Howard wasn't finished. "I think it might be good for us to assign a mentor for Suzanne. You know that church has destroyed several pastors."

One of the other men responded quickly. "No, I think that would take up valuable time which Rev. Hawkins needs for other things. Frankly, I think she should be doing the mentoring. Is there anything you need from us, Suzanne?"

"Not that I know of right now, but I surely will ask when and if I do."

"Very well then," Jan said. "Let's have a prayer. Howard, would you pray for her ministry?"

Tricky, tricky, Suzanne thought. She is really sharp. No wonder she's moderator of this complex and difficult committee.

" Most holy God, we praise you for all your good gifts. We ask you to look after Suzanne as she serves you in a difficult place. Give her energy, intelligence, imagination and love. And keep her safe in your care. In Jesus' name we pray. Amen."

# CHAPTER 22

MILDRED handed Suzanne a stack of newspaper clippings while she unlocked the door of a room behind the fellowship hall. "This used to be the Boy Scout Room but they needed a bigger one so it became mine. Here we are. Just put those papers on the table."

She turned on the overhead fluorescent lights. Suzanne expected filing cabinets, but what she saw was a small parlor. Two ancient pulpit chairs, intricately carved, their green velvet seats worn clear through in spots, sat on either side of a claw-footed table. Ornate shelves above it held chalices, Bibles, and a large poster entitled "The Welsh Language." Pictures on the walls showed the humble buildings of the three congregations which joined together and formed Covenant Presbyterian.

"Mildred, do people remember which church they came from? Is that a source of division?"

"They remember all right, but I don't think it's a problem. Look, over here are our former pastors."

Gloomy men stared ahead in their formal portraits, and Mildred pointed out an empty spot in the line up. "Somebody stole Rev. Terry a long time ago. Nobody ever fessed up to it. After that, we decided to keep all the photographs in here.

"Now, look at this." She unlocked a large closet. Three filing cabinets lined the right wall and held boxes on top. Beside them toward the back stood a tall metal cabinet. Across the back wall floor-to-ceiling shelves held record books, old hymnals, photograph albums, and objects in silvercloth bags. "This is where our silver is kept.

"Sit down here." Mildred pointed Suzanne to one pulpit chair, and she sat in the other. One by one she went through albums of pictures. Suzanne thought she'd nod off from boredom and lack of air. But then people she knew appeared.

"Here are Tommy and Catherine. Let's see, they married in twenty-eight so this would be 1930 or so. I have a picture of Liz at a young age somewhere." She flipped through the album. "Here it is. This is her mother's funeral. She was about fourteen. There's one of her and Rose back here." She flipped through pages. "Look, this is back when Liz and Rose were just babies toddling around."

"Did you put all these albums together?" Suzanne asked.

She took a moment to answer, her eyes moving from the pictures to Suzanne as though returning to the present day. "Yes, everyone gives me their memorabilia."

"Here are some other pictures of Rose. This is her baptism." The wide-eyed baby held in Bronwen's arms wore a long, lacy gown. John stood beside them, smiling, his eyes locked on the child.

"Is that Tommy and Catherine with them?"

"Yes, they were her godparents as well as her aunt and uncle. Now, this one here was taken about a year before Rose died." The beautiful girl from Bronwen's painting stood cheek to cheek with a grinning tomboyish Liz. Beside that photograph was another of the same pose, but Rose had been cut out leaving Liz beside John and Bronwen. That's a little strange, Suzanne thought.

"They were typical teenagers," Mildred said. "Up and down. Of course, the summer after this was taken, Rose died and Liz's mother Helen did, too. That was tragic. But Rose... I never told anyone else this," she whispered, "but I think that was a blessing. The girl wasn't right, you know. What would have become of her? I thought everybody was going to be better off, but Bronwen has never been the same. John recovered from it, and I think Catherine did, too. She may have seen it the way I did. But Tommy—God bless him. He mourned that girl something awful. You'd have thought she was his own child. Of course, he and Catherine never had children. I have my suspicions about that—you know she was always sickly.

"I used to wonder what would have happened if Liz hadn't had any other family when her mother died. It would have been perfect for Bronwen to take her in. The girls were the same age. Bronwen and John could have had a normal family."

"What happened to Liz's father?"

"He was a drunk. Drank himself to an early grave. But Liz had her grandmother. If you ask me, Anna saved that girl then and then again when Liz's husband left her."

When Mildred reached for another album, Suzanne said, "This is a strange little room, but it looks like a safe place for all this history. Is it fireproof?"

"I think so unless the fire started in here. It's also a good room to go to if a tornado is coming, the best place in town. Underground, no windows."

"I'll remember that."

"But I have the key. I'm the only one with a key to this room." She shook her key ring and winked. "Not even the pastor gets one. But I come over here and ride out bad storms, so I've got you covered. Waiting for a storm to pass over is a good time to look through the old books."

"Thank you, Mildred, but that's all I can take in today."

"Well, okay," she said, pursing her lips.

* * *

As they walked back upstairs, Suzanne asked, "Have you seen Tommy lately? I need to go by there and see how he's doing."

133

"Oh, yes, I'm keeping him busy. We like to watch wrestling to-gether. He's old, but he's not dead, you know." She giggled. "Say, are you going to see JJ today?"

"I don't think so. Why?"

"I was just wondering."

\* \* \*

As soon as Mildred left, Suzanne turned to Liz, "We need to have a key made for the history room."

# CHAPTER 23

ON St. David's Day, the first Sunday in March, Suzanne, Julie and Peter were eating lunch in the library when the door burst open.

"People are looking everywhere for you," Mildred said. Suzanne had her mouth full of pizza. Julie and Peter stared at the sight. Mildred wore a stovepipe hat and a bright red and black checked shawl. "People are here. They want to meet you."

Suzanne swallowed quickly. "But it's only twelve-thirty. Doesn't the celebration start at two?"

"Yes, yes, yes, but people are here. They come real early to get a seat."

Suzanne followed Mildred to the sanctuary. She stopped short in surprise as they rounded the corner. People crowded into the narthex and were beginning to fill up the sanctuary. She never imagined she'd see the church this full of people.

Some women wore hats similar to Mildred's, black with a stiff brim and a tall cylinder, which reminded Suzanne of Abraham Lincoln's top hat. They wore shawls and aprons, too. Most of the men looked like they always did, although a few wore formal suits and ties.

The guest conductor, however, wore a green bow tie and green velvet jacket with brass buttons and a plaid vest. He produced a daffodil for Suzanne and beamed as he pinned it on her. "This, my dear, is the flower of the day. 'Tis a great joy for me to be with you," he said in his sweet rolling accent.

"Our pastor has Welsh background, too," Mildred said. "Here, here I got this for you," she said to Suzanne as she pinned it on her. It was a green circle with a red dragon and letters which said, "I'm proud to be Welsh, CYMRU."

* * *

After the prelude by a guest harpist, the crowd sang "The Star Spangled Banner" and then the Welsh National anthem, that one in Welsh. "Lusty" was the word for the singing. Suzanne stood in front of everyone with no clue how to read the Welsh words, which seemed to her to have too many consonants and not enough vowels. The last verse however was in English,

> Wales! Wales! Fav'rite land of Wales!
> 'Till death be past, my love shall last;
> My longing, my yearning for Wales.

Suzanne welcomed everyone and gave the invocation, then stepped down to join Julie and Peter in the front row. Notes passed back and forth from them and finally Suzanne intercepted one.

> "What are those hats for?"
> "That's where they keep their candy."
> "I think they have rabbits under their hats."
> "No, they're drums."

She gave them what they called "the eye" and they stopped.

The choir sang familiar Welsh hymns, some with the congregation. Suzanne was surprised how many of her favorites in the hymnbook were Welsh. The director sang two beautiful, emotional solos.

And the program ended with everyone singing Cwm Rhonda, "Guide Me O Thou Great Jehovah."

The booming voices behind her in the congregation and in front of her in the chorus swept Suzanne up in what the conductor described as "the language of heaven." She found the music to be spiritual and expressive of a deep longing. She loved it. Her grandmother had said that music gave her the only acceptable expression of deep emotion. Suzanne agreed.

\* \* \*

Avoiding the crowds of people, Suzanne slipped down the back stairs to the fellowship hall where Mildred waited for her.

"Mildred, have you been to Wales?"

"Lord, no. I've never been further than Topeka," she said with pride.

"Do you know if anyone in the church has?"

"Not that I know of. Now, come, look at what I've done." Along the side walls and across the back of the room, tables and room dividers displayed pictures, books and other memorabilia from the history room. "See," Mildred said, "I've arranged everything in order. Over there I put the oldest pictures and Bibles, then..."

Suzanne tuned out, distracted by people beginning to enter and go to the table for tea. Mildred noticed them, too. "Come over here. This is where you should sit, close to the serving table. People can come to you because you'd never get around to see everyone. I'll get you some tea."

Bronwen sat nearby, serving tea and bread. "This is my great grandmother's recipe for bara brith," she told Suzanne, handing her a plate. "Every family has its own secret way of making it." The fruity flavors and the delicate crust left Suzanne wanting more.

Bronwen introduced Suzanne to those from out of town, helping her make connections with the extended family of Covenant Church.

One man who had come from New Mexico dragged Suzanne through the crowd over to the history display to point out his ancestors. Others were doing the same, many with children. Several gathered around Anna who was telling Liz and Buddy a story about the old days.

When Suzanne returned to her table, Bronwen said, "It's up to Anna, The Colonel and Mildred to pass on the stories now. And we need to learn all we can."

Bronwen's face looked younger and relaxed, more like her pictures before Rose died.

Nevertheless, Suzanne saw in her eyes the toll grief had taken. Her heart warmed and melted for Bronwen and the people around her, as she sat in the midst of their shared history of joys and sufferings. Community, she thought. This is community.

\* \* \*

JJ spotted her and rushed over with his arms full. "Ah, Milady Pastor, would you do me the honor of wearing Great Aunt Edith's finery?"

He held out a beautiful silk paisley shawl, as big as a blanket and put it around her shoulders. Out of a box, he pulled a stovepipe hat and a white ruffled bonnet. "Here you put this bonnet on first and then the hat."

People began taking pictures of her and JJ. Peter and Julie punched each other and burst into wild laughter. She didn't care. She liked feeling tall for a change.

And she felt like the queen of something, sitting there next to the serving table wearing the hat and the beautiful shawl. People did indeed come to greet her or to be introduced.

They told her of their family connections, pointed out pictures and bragged about ancestors.

I love being a pastor, she thought. There's never a dull moment. And at times like this their deep connections include me. I am blessed.

*  *  *

That night, she described the day to Bell. "You should have come," she said. "It was an amazing experience to see the joy they have in their heritage. And I've learned a lot about being of Welsh descent, too."

"Suz, you know you're getting too close to these people, don't you?" Bell said. "I think you're losing all objectivity."

She put down the family calendar they had finished filling in for the next week. "What do you mean? My goal is to establish relationships."

"You're getting too close. You talk like you are one of them instead of their leader."

# CHAPTER 24

"Look, look, you're in the newspaper." Liz greeted her on Monday morning. There on the front page, she and JJ looked like folk dancers. "That will get you marks from everyone in town. Don't you look cute?" Then in a whisper, she said, "Guess who took my grandmother out to dinner last night."

"I can't imagine," Suzanne said.

"I've been dying to tell you. The Colonel invited her to dinner after yesterday's festival. She said they had a good time talking and laughing about old times and all the St. David's Day festivals they've been to. But I don't think we'd better tell Mildred. She'll be livid. Oops, is that gossip?"

"I think we'd call it good news. After all, there's a hint of spring in the air." Suzanne said. "I wonder if I should put off my visit with Tommy for a few days. He may think I'm there to pry." She smiled thinking about those two having a good time.

\* \* \*

As it turned out, she didn't have time to go see Tommy anyway. Morgan called. "I need to talk to you. Is there any chance you could come for lunch today?" The young woman, an elder, had impressed Suzanne with her wisdom and courage as they discussed matters at the session meetings. Liz said she was the smartest and most creative person she knew. She taught junior high math and also co-owned a health food store.

* * *

The mailbox stood in front of a trailer where a goat lounged in the doorway. A chicken flew at its head, but the goat sat as serene as a Buddha in the early spring sunshine. Suzanne doubled-checked the address on the mailbox against her note.

She knocked on the door of the next trailer, prepared to ask directions to Morgan's house, but the young woman opened the door. Her eyes blinked at the bright light, and she looked confused for a moment. "Pastor, come in. Excuse me. I was deep into meditation and didn't realize what time it was. She wore a flowing blue caftan and her hair hung in a long braid down her back. Beyond her sat a low table which held incense, candles, and a brass bowl.

She led Suzanne to her kitchen table. "Here, sit down, cup of tea? It's honeysuckle and mint from the yard—helps clear the mind."

Suzanne breathed in deeply the flavorful steam. It smelled like springtime.

"Now," Morgan said standing at the stove. "I have three things on my mind. First, I'm pregnant. Due in July. I was raped back a few weeks before you came or I would have told you. But I'm okay."

"Have you seen a crisis counselor?" Suzanne asked.

Morgan held her hands up as though stopping traffic. "I'm okay. I've dealt with it and this will be my baby. I don't know who it was and I don't want to. This will be my baby. But I need help figuring out what to tell the congregation. Actually, it's more complicated because—." She held up two fingers.

"The second thing on my mind is that I want to get married in June. His name is Ralph. We've been friends a long time, and he knows what happened. He wants to marry me and raise this baby as his own. And I'm sure I want to be married to him. We've talked

142

about all the complexities until it doesn't seem complex any more." She put the teacups down and with a sweet, soft smile sat down across from Suzanne.

"Third—" Suzanne held her breath. My God, what more could there be?

"Ralph's uncle is burning some of his prairie tonight. Do you want to go?"

"Wow, Morgan, you've got a lot going on. Let's take the third one first. What's this about burning the prairie?"

"Every spring we set fire to the prairie to get rid of weeds. And it puts nutrients back into the ground, too. Then the beautiful grasses can flourish. It's quite a sight, and we thought you'd enjoy it. It's also a chance to meet Ralph. Oh, I didn't say, but we'd like you to do the wedding, of course, unless that would cause you trouble in the church."

Suzanne took in a long breath willing her body to relax. "First, I'd be happy to marry you two. Second, you sound like you've made up your mind how to think about the baby in a healthy way, but if you need to talk it through again now or in our marriage counseling or in the future, I'll be available. Third, is the fire safe?"

"Yes, it's very controlled. The wind has to be just right, enough to carry the fire but not so much it will move too fast. There are men all along the fire line controlling where it travels."

"I'd love to see that," Suzanne said. "Now, let's talk about numbers one and two, a baby and a wedding. Are you wondering which to do first?"

"No, I've decided to get married before the baby comes. Then it will be Ralph's baby. And I've thought about how big I'll be, too. But I intend to have the wedding I've always dreamed of anyway. Tell me what you think about this. I'm counting on you to tell me if this is inappropriate. I picture a white gown with a v-neck." She stood and demonstrated as she talked. "The bodice will be very fitted but empire style and the dress will flow from that point into a complete circle at the bottom with several poufs kind of like a bustle all the way around, or maybe three or four tiers, and a long train of tiny poufs. I haven't quite decided on that." She took a deep breath. "What do you think?"

"My opinion is that it is your wedding and you can do anything you want. The only requirements for me to do it is that it be Christian, that it be a worship service in which you make your vows before God and God's people. And whatever you do should be in keeping with worship of God."

"Good! We had a minister once who had a whole passel of rules about weddings. But what do you think about white?"

"Whose opinion are you concerned about?"

There was a long pause.

"I don't know. I just don't want to offend the church... or you. And I don't want to be a laughingstock."

"You can't control other people. Let's talk about what you will be comfortable with. Does wearing white bother you?"

Morgan took two plates out of the refrigerator. "No, even if I cared about that tradition, I consider myself a virgin whether anyone else does or not."

"Okay. That's settled. What else?"

"The dress, do you think it will work?"

"Have you seen one like you described?"

"No, I'm going to make it myself."

"I've seen one with scalloped poufs like you describe. Each one looked as though it were held up by a little bow."

"That might look better. I'm going to do some sketches and maybe I'll make one out of muslin before I do the final so I can make changes. Okay, that's helpful. Now, here's some goat cheese, some blueberries from last year's crop. And this is bulgur bread I made this morning."

"Looks good. Did you make the goat cheese, too?"

"Yes, I guess you saw my livestock. The goats love that trailer, the chickens, too. The chickens keep telling the goats to leave, but they pay no attention to them.

"Now, I wonder, what do you think about how much I should tell the congregation and when?"

"You don't have to tell the congregation anything. But the question is will you feel like you're keeping a secret that will bother you? Or are you okay with them thinking the baby is yours and Ralph's conceived before marriage? What will you feel most at peace about now and then later as the child grows up? Another consideration is what will Ralph be most comfortable with?"

"We have talked about some of that but not all of it. Those are some good questions. We'll spend some time on them. Thanks."

\* \* \*

Later, as Suzanne drove herself and Morgan over the gentle, rolling hills to meet Ralph, she asked Morgan, "How did you and Ralph meet?"

"I've volunteered for years at the Land Institute where he works, and we've done projects together."

"What's the Land Institute?"

She looked over sharply. "You never heard of it? It's in Salina, outside of town a bit." She paused. "Well, you've only been there—how long?

"A year and a half," Suzanne said.

Morgan looked out over the grass-covered hills. "The Land Institute conducts important research into sustainable crops. If we don't stop annual plowing and chemical usage, we will lose the productivity of our land. Wes Jackson—have you heard of him?"

Suzanne had to admit to another failure.

"Wes Jackson is a genius. He founded the Land Institute and

is the head of it. He's going to lead us into growing grains that are perennials. They will reseed themselves. Anyway, Ralph will talk your ear off about it if you let him. We're both fanatics. Now I understand what you said about how beautiful the wheat is and how much you like to watch the cattle on the hills, but if you say that to Ralph, you're liable to hear more than you ever wanted to know about what has ruined the natural prairie."

"Okay," Suzanne said, glad for the warning. "This land is beautiful in the twilight. Are these what people call the Flint Hills?"

"Yes, they're full of limestone, flinty limestone. The early settlers couldn't plow through it. Elk and bison grazed them, but now there are only a few places where you can see untouched prairie. I think the Flint Hills are beautiful, too. I've always thought they were magical, especially at this time of evening. My granddad used to tell me he rode in a wagon down one of those hills and went so fast that the wagon kept going up the next hill and down and up and kept on like that for three days. He also told me in the early days the grass was so tall you couldn't see a man on horseback. That part is true."

Suzanne laughed. She could imagine such talk as she admired the golden brown hills, their gentle round crowns and valleys rolling away as far as she could see. To her they looked like waves you could ride to the ends of the earth.

"Look," Morgan said as they reached the top of a hill. "See the fire? Pull over here and flash your lights a few times. Ralph will find us."

Suzanne caught her breath. "Oh, my. I had no idea." A snake of fire ran from a crevice at the bottom of the hill in front of them and off into the distance. It spit up golden flames as it ate the grass and wound around and over hills across the prairie. She saw a man in a jeep, and others walking along the line of fire.

She and Morgan got out and leaned against the car. Smoke wafted toward them on the wind. The sun dropped over the far hills turning them soft shades of purple and gold. Sky and prairie slowly moved together and deepened in color, their undulations as soothing as a lullaby accompanied by the crackling of burning grass and the whoosh of gentle winds.

* * *

Ralph drove up in a jeep and jumped out, his eyes on the fire until Morgan introduced him. He wore a John Deere cap and had a smudge on his nose."It's burning well tonight," he said. "You see, Pastor, we've got to protect the prairie. These fires help the native grasses grow by burning off the duff, that's dead stems and leaves. Then the grasses under the ground feel the warmth of the spring sun and start to grow. You know, the tallgrasses can grow six to eight feet high." He went on and on telling her about the long-lived perennials, "perhaps hundreds of years old" and the forbs, "that's prairie wildflowers."

Suzanne had to finally cut him off. "Ralph, I've got to get home. This has been a magical evening. Thank you for inviting me, and I look forward to performing your marriage ceremony. If you'll call the office and make three appointments, we'll talk everything through."

He and Morgan looked at each other with obvious delight. And he finally let Suzanne go after only a few "one more thing I want to tell you" moments. Suzanne opened her car door. "One more thing," he said, "if this wedding would cause you trouble at church, please let us know. We don't want to put more pressure on you than you've already got. On the other hand, we might take the attention and heat off you." He grinned.

Suzanne left the couple and drove home in the dark, watching the thin line of fire curl around the hills as long as she could.

# Chapter 25

Spring flowers, spring sunshine, and spring lightness of spirit touched Middletown and Covenant Presbyterian Church. The Session's okay for the youth choir's mission project blossomed into a joy for the congregation. On Sunday afternoons ten to twelve children of differing shades of skin gathered in the fellowship hall with youth choir members and four faithful adults. They worked together on homework assignments and then had refreshments and played games. Church members began to brainstorm about how to meet other needs the children had and talked about teaching their parents to read. To Suzanne's delight the elders began to speak of it as "our tutoring program."

Liz began asking in mid-March for holy week information so she could get all the worship bulletins ready. Four services in one week put pressure on all the staff. They had to plan Palm Sunday and then Maundy Thursday and Good Friday and finally Easter. Suzanne worked late several days to get those services ready so Liz could type and print them. She also worked ahead to have everything ready for the week after Easter when she was taking vacation days to go the lake with the Edwards family. Ed and Jewell had invited her and her family to join them for the "Opening of the Cottage."

Maundy Thursday the congregation celebrated a Seder meal and reminder of how Jesus changed it to his Last Supper. At Good Friday's Tenebrae service, the light dimmed with each of the seven last words until the sanctuary was dark. In silence they left Jesus alone on the black-draped cross.

Easter Sunday's chilly air didn't dampen rising spirits. White Easter lilies filled the front of the sanctuary. White paraments covered the communion table, pulpit and lectern. And Suzanne wore her white robe and stole, which featured gold sunbursts. At the beginning of the service the light-filled sanctuary echoed with antiphonal alleluias from half of the choir in the front and half in the back.

* * *

Finally, full of excitement, Suzanne, Peter and Julie followed the Edwards family to the lake. "Matt and Robert and their dad came out Friday afternoon and Saturday," Peter said. "Matt said his arms were sore this morning from all the work they did getting the cottage ready for summer."

When they drove up, Bell had already arrived at the cottage and was pulling fishing poles out of the trunk. "Dad, hey, Dad," Julie cried. "Look they have a boat." The sturdy stone house overlooked rippling water. Suzanne felt tension flowing out of her body.

After they unloaded everything, Ed gave them a tour. "The house is essentially one big living room with a bedroom on either side. You've seen your bedroom," he nodded to Bell and Suzanne. Jewell and I have an identical one on the other side of the house. This living room and those bedrooms make up the original house. Tommy added a kitchen on the back and a workshop beyond that. And he added bathrooms off each bedroom. Now, this fireplace—." He smiled. "This fireplace is original and one of a kind. Tommy's mother liked to cook over the open fire. These are her iron pots and implements." He pointed to the ladles, spoons and pans hanging from the mantle. "What do you think of that?" he asked Suzanne.

"It's beautiful, twice as big as any I've ever seen. Will we have a fire tonight?"

"Oh, yes, we sure will. It's the only heat we'll have. Tommy liked it that way. 'Cool enough to enjoy the hearth and warm the heart,' he always said. He used to gather everybody in the evenings to sing the old songs and tell stories. The first one up in the morning builds a roaring fire, and the rest of us sleep until it's warm."

"Who's Tommy?" Bell asked.

Jewell quickly apologized. "Bell, we didn't tell you that our host is The Colonel, Tommy Lewis. You probably saw the post rock out front with Lewis on it. His father built this cottage way back when he was a young man."

"We're the only ones who use it now," Ed said. "Not even Tommy's brother John and Bronwen come out any more. We open it in the spring and take care of it all summer and close it up again in the late fall."

Jewell took over the story. "Tommy and his wife Catherine and Mary—that's the woman who takes care of them—loved to come here until Catherine got too ill. John and Bronwen came, too. We had some great times. Most of the summer our family and theirs would gather here in the evenings. Ed and I had a little cabin down the road a ways. We girls would swim during the day and enjoy the sun while the men fished."

"Here, Bell, are those Julie's things?" Jewell said. "They go out on the porch. She and Sarah will sleep over there." She pointed to a corner of the screened porch, which spanned the front of the house. "Matt and Peter will sleep in the tent with Robert. It's set up back by the workshop."

"It's a big tent," Robert said. "Let's get your stuff and I'll show you."

"Okay, now, you all settle in," Jewell said. "I'll get our Easter dinner ready. I expect everyone's getting hungry."

Ed started singing and the children joined in as they dispersed carrying their bedding and clothes with them, "Here we sit like birds in the wilderness, birds in the wilderness, birds in the wilderness. Here we sit like birds in the wilderness, waiting for our food."

Suzanne and Jewell set out food on the long refectory table, which stretched across one side of the living room from the kitchen to the front wall of the house. Bell sliced the smoked ham and turkey he had brought and added it to the table already full with potato salad from Suzanne (her mother's recipe), Jewell's green bean casserole, and homemade rolls.

Ed asked the blessing on the food. "Gracious God, grant us your mercy as we indulge ourselves. Bless this food and us to thy service."

"Leave room for caramel cake and homemade ice cream," Jewell said.

* * *

Later the children brought out blankets and floor pillows from the closet and cuddled up on the rug in front of the fire. Jewell, Bell and Suzanne sat on the oversized soft couch leaving the ancient leather chair and footstool for Ed. Robert brought up a chair from the dining room table, and the circle was complete. Yawns accompanied the crackle of the fire, and Suzanne assumed they'd all be headed for bed soon.

But Ed started telling stories and soon had them all laughing. "Ol' Robbie went to the cemetery with all the boys to bury Gerry and when the service was finished, his friend says to him, 'Ho, ol' Robbie, you're not lookin' so good, you're not. Do you think it's worth the trip for you to go back into town?'"

When the story telling wound down, Sarah asked, "Can we go swimming tomorrow?"

"Why, sure you can go swimming," Ed said. "Bell and I will head out early to catch those wily fish, but not too early." He wiggled his bushy eyebrows at Bell. "Just be sure one of the adults is here watching while you swim."

"Aw, Dad," she said. "We're old enough to take care of ourselves."

"Not if those gotcha fish find you," he said grabbing her leg with his feet. She squealed and threw a pillow at him.

"Peter and I want to make something in the workshop," Matt said.

"Now, that for sure needs supervision," Jewell said. "Lots of fingers have been lost on equipment like that."

"That's some workshop," Bell said. "I saw a circular saw, a jigsaw... what else?" "There's a lathe," Robert said.

"The lathe, that's what I want to use to make something," Matt said.

"There's a router, too," Ed said. "Tommy used to make some beautiful furniture." He looked around. "He made that table over there and the ones in the bedrooms. And probably more things in here that I'm not aware of."

"How about I show you what's in the shop and what each one is used for," Robert said. "We can do that in the morning while the old men are fishing, before it gets warm enough to swim. But I'm not sure you want to go swimming. The water's still pretty cold."

The girls groaned. "We'll try it," Sarah said.

"I'd like to go see the wildflowers in the morning." Jewell looked at Suzanne. "Want to come?"

"Sure. What wildflowers are there?"

"I'm not sure I can remember any of their names. Rose knew them all. I think of it as her wildflower garden. It's just down past the cabin we used to own. There's a stand of trees and a field."

"Mom," Sarah said. "It seems like nobody likes to talk about Rose. What's the mystery?"

"It's a sad memory. She was only fourteen when she died. Such a tragedy."

"How did she die?" Peter asked.

Before Jewell could answer, Ed blurted out, "She died in the workshop, hit her head on the corner of one of those—." He waved his hand and coughed.

Peter exchanged horror faces with Matt.

"Mom, would it make you too sad to tell us about her?" Sarah asked.

"I wish you could have known her," Jewell said. "She was extraordinary, like a bright light. When she was around I felt almost mesmerized by her beauty and her love. She enhanced our enjoyment by the delight she took in everything around her: birds, flowers, animals, even rocks. Ed loved to take her picture. For a long time he displayed my favorite one in the window of his shop downtown. Then he gave it to Bronwen."

"Ed's a photographer," Suzanne told Bell. "I don't know if you knew that."

Jewell went on, "When she was a baby, she looked like one of those perfect baby dolls you have, Sarah—creamy skin, long eyelashes, big brown eyes, pink cheeks. And as she grew, she became another beautiful doll, a bigger one. Remember the doll you had that could walk? She was like that, still beautiful, just a bigger baby doll. She could have been a beauty queen. But her mind didn't grow."

"Who were her parents?" Bell asked.

"Oh, sorry, Bell. Bronwen and John Lewis, and her aunt and uncle were Catherine and Tommy Lewis."

"John and Tommy are half-brothers. Tommy's a lot older though," Ed added.

"That's a very sad story," Julie said.

"It was devastating," Jewell said. "Like the lights turned off in Bronwen and John's lives. Tommy and Catherine's, too. And Mary's. Their lives revolved around Rose. Their spirits never recovered."

"It was hard for us, too," Ed said. "There was never anyone else like Rose." He paused. "But now we're here filling this house with laughter again. We're glad you're all here, and tomorrow we'll have fun fishing, swimming, and cutting fingers off."

"I noticed a board on the porch is starting to crack," Bell said. "Maybe we could get the boys to help us replace it."

\* \* \*

It's been a long day and a long week, Suzanne thought as she snuggled up to Bell that night. He must be cold, she thought, because he didn't move away as he usually did, claiming to be too hot. The girls giggled on the screened porch, and then all was silent. She listened to the water lapping. This is a good tired, a good Easter tired. Now we have a whole week with no phone calls, no television, and no responsibilities.

\* \* \*

"Suze, Suze, let's get up and watch the sun rise," Bell whispered.

They tiptoed over the squeaky wood floors to light the fire and then sneaked out to the dock to sit and watch the light build across the water. No hills or trees obscured the view. Light radiated from below the horizon, turning the sky from dark grey to lighter grey to pink.

"Don't blink or you'll miss it," Bell said. And sure enough, one millisecond it wasn't there and the next the tip of the golden ball peeked at them and the sky around it changed from pink to rose, the water from grey blue to purple. Sunrise. "It came up again!" Bell shouted.

"Coffee," Suzanne yelled and raced him to the house.

The whole week was carefree. It was fun. They cooked a pot of soup in the fireplace. They played hearts in the evenings and sang. They opened a large cupboard, which was full of musical instruments, including kazoos and tambourines. Robert played the recorder, Jewell the accordion, and Ed the fiddle.

I haven't had fun in a long time, Suzanne thought. And I haven't seen Bell like this since... since I don't know when. I wonder if it's genuine or an attempt to avoid seeing a counselor.

Another morning as they watched the sunrise, Bell put his arm around her, held her close and kissed her forehead. "This is the way God intended his people to enjoy life," he said.

# CHAPTER 26

"Did he call you, too?" Suzanne asked as she entered Tommy's den and saw JJ standing at the window with his back to her. He turned from watching the gardener trim a misshapen antler on a deer bush.

"Yes, do you know what it's about?" He gave her a big hug.

"Not a clue."

They watched the gardener carefully shape the bushes. Eight days ago I had not a care in the world, sitting on the dock watching the clouds, she thought. It only takes a couple of days to get overburdened again.

Jesus said, "Come to me all you who are heavily burdened and I will give you rest." How soon, O Lord, how soon will rest come again?

JJ said, "I can't figure out why he would summon both of us. I feel like I've been called to the principal's office."

The door burst open and Tommy strode in as much as a man with a cane can stride.

"Hey there," JJ said. "How are you getting along?"

His pleasant greeting was met with a grunt as Tommy picked out a cigar and waved it at them. "It has come to my attention that you two have been seeing each other. What were you thinking? The church can't handle a scandal. If this ends up destroying us, I will hold you two responsible."

"No, no," JJ said. "It's not like that."

Tommy pointed his cigar at him. "No excuses. It's all over town." He turned to Suzanne. "You have to do the right thing here. The longer you stay the worse it will be for us."

Suzanne opened her mouth, but no words came to her.

The more JJ tried to explain, the louder Tommy talked. Finally, there was nothing to do but leave.

JJ broke the awkward silence. He and Suzanne stood at the street in front of Tommy's house.

"Had lunch?" he said.

It brought Suzanne out of her shock and whirling thoughts. "You vote for defiance?"

"You bet," he said. "Let's go talk strategy."

She teared up.

"How this appeared to other people never entered my mind. I'm so sorry, Suzanne," he said, echoing her thoughts. "I'm angry and ready to lash out, but again I'm not considering your position."

"Should we let such gossip control us?" she asked.

"My immediate reaction is no. If we stop meeting for lunch, we'll look guilty. If we don't, your work with the church may be compromised or made much more difficult.We can fight it, give in to it or ignore it. I'll do what you want to. I don't think I'll lose business over this, but your product might suffer." He winked.

"I'm not sure what to do, JJ."

"Meet me at my house. I'll fix sandwiches, and we can talk about it," JJ said.

* * *

She'd never before seen his private rooms at the Funeral Home. Whoever had decorated the square kitchen made it overly cheerful with a tablecloth that matched the wallpaper's cherries and oranges. Suzanne felt queasy looking at it.

"Let's sit by the fire," JJ suggested, and they carried their ham and swiss sandwiches and coffee to the parlor. He lit the fire and turned on the dim light of the floor lamp.

Suzanne set the coffee on the table next to her chair and tucked her legs up under her. She couldn't focus. Her eyes wanted to close and give in to the warmth.

The phone rang. She heard JJ in the next room making arrangements to pick up someone's dearly departed. While he talked, she ate. She carried her empty plate to the kitchen and got another cup of coffee. When she returned to the parlor, he walked in. "Sorry about that," he said. "Are you okay?" She stood in the middle of the room and turned toward the kitchen then back to the chair, unsure where she was going. "You look dazed."

Tears fell onto her hand before she realized she was crying. "I don't know. I don't know what to do. I was warned this congregation was difficult, but people have geen so nice to me, I am shocked. And I haven't done anything to warrant this kind of accusation. I may not be able to convince people. Without their trust—."

He took her into his arms and patted her on the back. "I'm so sorry. I'm so sorry. We'll figure this out. It will be okay," he said.

The fire warmed her. His chin sat on top of her head. She felt safe. She believed him.

\* \* \*

Later at her desk, she felt guilty. Should I feel guilty? she asked herself. I haven't done anything wrong... unless JJ has read into this more than I have. He's always been so easy and fun to be with, I've never given a thought about how it looked.

\* \* \*

Before Suzanne could call Bell, he called her.

"Are you all right?" he asked. "We received a call in the office saying you were in trouble. The woman hung up before we could find out who it was."

"There are rumors going around that JJ and I are spending time together. 'Seeing each other,' is the phrase Tommy used. You know who JJ is? The funeral director. We've become good friends. We often walk to lunch together so I guess it's pretty visible and somebody got the wrong idea. I never thought anything of it."

"Someone may have intentionally skewed this to cause you trouble," he said and paused. "Is there any more to it than that?"

"No, not at all. He reminds me of my best friend in grade school." And I hope he feels that way, she thought. She did enjoy JJ and look forward to their lunches. Their discussions ranged from her sermon plans to books they'd read and anything else on their minds. He was a good listener, and he made her laugh.

Her relationship with Bell, though not as affectionate as she would like, had improved after the Christmas trip to Alabama and the time at the lake after Easter. We need time like that when we're our own little family, not part of his church family or mine, she thought. We probably need more time for just the two of us, too. But surely he won't believe these rumors.

"Bell, what do you think I should do?"

"Stop going to lunch with him."

She waited a beat. "I'll think about that. But wouldn't I look guilty if I do that and give into the lies?"

"No, just stop going to lunch with him, and it'll all blow over."

\* \* \*

In a similar phone call, Sadie suggested a session meeting to bring all of it out in the open. "Surely, that is giving this too much attention," Suzanne said, but Sadie insisted, and Suzanne agreed to think about it.

She talked it over with Bell that evening as they changed into comfortable clothes before dinner. "Sadie said their dysfunction would surely come to the forefront in my relationship with them and theirs with me. I guess this is it. She said rumors will go on and on unless a clear face down happens publicly. She proposes to invite anyone who wants to come so that there is no room for conjecture."

"It's not right," he said. "It's unfair to let your personal life be laid out for people to tromp on."

"It is unfair that we're at the mercy of opinions and perceptions. Where is there room for truth?"

"Amen," he said. "Keep strong and hold onto that attitude. You're cute when you get all feisty."

She rolled her eyes at him.

\* \* \*

Bell insisted on being there if such a meeting happened. Peter and Julie overheard them. "We should be there, too," Peter said.

Suzanne said, "Absolutely not."

However, on Friday night, as they sat at a table in front of The Ice Cream Parlor in downtown Salina, Bell asked them why they wanted to go.

Peter was concentrating on his dripping ice cream cone. Julie said, "I'm a member of the church, and if all members are invited, then I should be allowed to go, too. I want to know what's going on. You're my mother. I should be there." She hesitated. "You know if what they're saying is true, we'll love you anyway."

"What? What are they saying?"

Peter looked down, but Julie looked her in the eye. "They're saying you're gay," she said.

Suzanne's ice cream melted down over her hand as she stared at her daughter, trying to comprehend this. Even the children are hearing rumors, she thought.

Bell coughed, then snorted. And Suzanne joined him in a long, hearty belly laugh.

"Why is this happening?" she wondered out loud wiping her hand with the minuscule napkin and accepting everyone else's napkin as well. "Why would anyone say these things about me? That is so totally off the wall. Surely no one really thinks... So why—."

Peter took a deep breath. "So you're not?"

"No, I'm not having an affair. I'm not gay. You can put your minds at rest. And if we have such a meeting, you can both come. You've already heard more rumors than we have."

Suzanne continued to mull it over. Where did someone get the idea that I am gay? Or maybe they spread that rumor to get rid of me since Presbyterian clergy couldn't be... oh, what are the words? "Self–affirming, practicing homosexuals." Every year when the General Assembly met, news reports sensationalized the matter and people in the pews got upset.

However, the only time homosexuality had come up at church was at the session meeting when Morgan gave her speech about one in eight men being homosexual and then told about the woman she knew who was abandoned when she told her best friend that her son was dying of AIDS. Morgan had courageously stood up for what she believed was right, but they didn't discuss the issue. It was simply an example of a headier issue they might have to discuss sometime. Morgan had said more than was called for in that moment, and Suzanne was slow to realize she should stop her.

Surely, nobody else knew about the other private discussion she'd had besides the one with Peter. Robert had come to her office one Sunday afternoon when nobody else was around. Rather tentatively, he sat down. She had the distinct impression that he wasn't sure he wanted to be there.

"I need to ask your advice about something," he began. "I, uh, I want to know what you think about homosexuality."

"What I think about it?"

"Yes. Like is it inborn or is it caused by how parents raise a child?"

"As far as I know, there isn't agreement on that, but lots of studies are going on. I read an article about the search for a 'gay gene' that a person is born with. Others claim homosexuality comes to a man if he has a distant relationship with his father. Other people think it's a choice. I know that those who believe it is inborn use the word 'orientation.' Those who believe it is a choice, say 'preference.'"

"What do you think?" he asked.

"My best guess is that it's inborn. My psychology professor in college said that each of us is born somewhere on a continuum of sexual attraction. He said we're all more or less attracted to each person we meet. My guess is that comes close to the truth. But in a few years scientists will know more about the genetics of it."

"That's sort of what Mr. Lewis said. My dad suggested I talk to him since he teaches psychology at the college. He said something like that."

"What do you think, Robert?"

"I think it's inborn, but I know not everyone does."

"Are you concerned about yourself or someone else?" she asked. Is he going to tell me Peter might be gay?

"I know that I'm gay. I've known for a long time," he said. "But I haven't told anyone except my dad and Mr. Lewis. The real question I have is whether to tell my mother, or maybe when to tell her. I can't keep this secret forever."

"What's holding you back from talking about this with her?"

"She's such a good mother, very sensitive about doing right by us kids, and I don't want to disappoint her. She might think it's her fault, that somehow she raised me to be this way."

\* \* \*

Peter and Julie's whispering brought Suzanne's attention back to her ice cream. They got up from the table and began walking to the car. She and Bell hurriedly finished and joined them.

"Mom," Julie said, "we have a surprise for you at home."

"An early birthday present," Peter added.

"Well, let's get on home. What is it?" she asked.

Julie giggled. "No, no guesses, no hints. You'll have to wait."

Once they got home, Julie and Peter disappeared upstairs to return with a small box wrapped in blue foil and white ribbon. "They wrapped it at the store," Julie said.

Inside she found a delicate gold cross with a rose engraved in the center of it.

"We decided you needed it now," Peter said.

*  *  *

In the middle of the night, Suzanne woke up and couldn't go back to sleep. Her mind swirled in that half-consciousness. People are talking about me, they're trying to get rid of me, and they don't like me. Why would they treat me this way? I've only tried to love them and help the church get healthier.

In the morning, she told Bell, "I may need to quit to save the church. The rumors have gone so far I'm not sure there's any way to call them back."

"It does seem like the minute rumors start, momentum takes over," he said. "People jump on the bandwagon and take sides, talking about all the reasons they like you or don't like you."

"That could split the church again," she said.

# CHAPTER 27

JJ stopped by the church. "Who do you think is starting rumors?" he asked as they fixed coffee in the kitchen.

"I try not to imagine who it is because then I become suspicious of everyone. But maybe I need to rethink that strategy."

He grinned. "Time to start protecting yourself instead of everyone else?"

"If you put it like that, it may be past time." She motioned him into her office and closed the door. "Do you have any idea who's doing this?"

"My mind automatically goes to Mildred Owens," he said, sitting down across from her at the table. "She delights in knowing everything that's going on."

"Have you ever known her to spread lies?"

"Not exactly lies," he said. "It's more like wild imaginings. She's a pistol."

"I don't think she'd do anything to hurt me," Suzanne said. "She's at the church most every day. She's pleasant and helpful. And I consider her a friend."

"Who else could it be?" JJ asked. "It's someone who talks to Tommy."

"I've noticed two men on the session who will occasionally say, 'The Colonel won't like it,' when we are deciding something. Of course, Mildred says that, too. But I haven't noticed decisions being made on that basis. It would make sense that it's someone who has stooped to this to get rid of me because he or she doesn't have power to do it through normal means."

"What would you do if you knew who it was?" he asked.

"I'd talk turkey to them."

"Would that change their behavior?"

"Probably not. Sadie, our Associate Executive in the Presbytery office, wants me to have a session meeting open to all members to discuss the rumors and how to stop them. I don't think that would do any good. It will simply spread them further and also give official recognition to them. The only way to keep the church from splitting up again is for me to leave."

* * *

She called Frances to get some support. After initial pleasantries, Suzanne told her what was happening.

Frances was silent for a moment and then said, "You know, don't you that there is more than one way to have an affair."

"But, I'm not—"

"Don't answer so quickly. Remember last year when Chet took some hits for preaching about nuclear weapons and found some comfort in "that woman"? You and Bell were really supportive and helpful to me. I'll never forget the time I spent with you in Kansas. Well, Chet said they hadn't had an affair, but our counselor said, 'There's more than one way to have an affair.' And she asked him some hard questions."

"This isn't like that. JJ and I are just good friends and we like talking to each other." Suzanne wondered if it had been a bad idea to call Frances, but her best friend from Ohio days had never let her down. She and Chet, both United Methodist pastors, shared much in common with Suzanne and Bell. When Chet had preached some social action sermons, the congregation asked Frances to preach more

166

and him less. It resulted in strain in their marriage. Since then, they started serving separate churches and their lives were back on an even keel.

"Suzanne, I'm not going to be hard on you, but, of course, I see this from Bell's point of view since I was standing in his shoes in the similar situation with Chet. But I'll tell you the questions if you want to hear them."

Suzanne took a deep breath. "Okay, let's hear them."

"The first one is, 'Did you tell your husband when you'd spent time with JJ?"

"I don't know. I don't think so. It didn't seem important."

"My counselor would say to that, 'It's important to spend time with this person, but not important enough to tell the most significant person in your life?"

"I think there could be exceptions to that," Suzanne said.

"Okay, do you want to hear more?"

"Yes."

"Do you spend more time with this other person than you do with your spouse?"

"Go on."

"Do you tell JJ things you don't tell Bell?"

"Do you talk with him about your difficulties with Bell?"

"That's a no."

"Do you look forward to being with him more than Bell?"

Suzanne was silent, and Frances went on.

"Do you talk to him from home?"

"Yes, but—"

"You don't have to answer to me," Frances said. "Has there been physical contact between you?"

"You mean like a hug?"

"You can answer that for yourself. There are hugs and there are hugs."

"Only a really good friend would talk to me like this," Suzanne said.

"I'm glad you see it that way. We've always been honest with each other. If there's nothing to this, you'll know. And if there is something there, you'll know that, too. You'll know what to do either way."

"Thanks, Frances. Our Presbytery Associate Executive says the dysfunction in the church will play out in their relationships with me. She thinks we should have a meeting to which everyone is invited and confront the gossip and rumors, see if we can bring the hurtful behavior into the light where everyone can see what's happening, and perhaps make a difference for this church's future. What do you think about that?"

"I think you have a wise woman helping you. I also think it would be good for Bell to be at that meeting if you have it. And you could think about opening the lunch time discussions to other people who want to come."

"Good thoughts, Frances. Thanks.

"Always remember you can come visit Chet and me in Ohio if you need to get away. I'm sending hugs for all of you. Happy birthday next week. My card will be late as usual."

Suzanne hung up and looked over the notes she had taken while Frances talked. Those are good questions to ask, she thought, but I can't see that I've done anything wrong.

# CHAPTER 28

SUZANNE sat down with Sadie Ross and Dr. Talley in his office in Salina. "I've thought long and hard about this," she said. "I've prayed about it, and it seems to me inevitable that at Covenant Church the church members are going to take sides. They probably already have started doing so. I think more people are going out the side doors after church on Sundays to avoid shaking hands. If I could prove the truth, it would be different, but I don't know how to do that."

"I understand," Sadie said, "but I'll say again that you have nothing to lose by having an open session meeting to discuss rumors. I'll drop it if you want me to, but I really think—.

After thoroughly exhausting the pros and cons of having such a meeting, Suzanne agreed that it was worth a try even though she doubted it would make much difference.

Dr. Talley said, "You are one of the most courageous people I know. You can do this."

\* \* \*

A week later thirty-five people sat around a large square of tables in the fellowship hall. "I've asked Sadie Ross to moderate this meeting," Suzanne said. "Most of you know that Sadie is the Associate Executive for Northern Kansas Presbytery. This is a called session meeting, open to members of the congregation, to address one item of business—rumors. Sadie will facilitate our discussion."

"Let's open this meeting with prayer," Sadie said. "Gracious God, we seek to glorify your loving presence. Your rod and staff comfort us, and we come to you with hearts open to your wisdom and guidance. Give us words, we pray, words of clarity and discernment for your will and your way. Amen.

"Let me be clear that my role is to objectively facilitate your discussion, not to influence it. This has been declared an open meeting to which any member of this church is welcome. We also have the Reverend Bell Hawkins, Pastor Suzanne's husband. He is not a member of this congregation, but is a minister member of this presbytery. Is there any objection to him observing?

"Hearing none, we'll move on. Now, permission to speak in this meeting is granted to members of the session whom you have elected to govern this congregation. Anyone else, who desires to speak, must be recognized by the chair (that's me). Make your request and we will ask the session to vote on that permission. This is used for reasons of order, not to stifle a viewpoint.

"I propose that we begin with a statement from Rev. Suzanne Hawkins, and then open the floor for discussion. Are there any questions or objections about how we will proceed?"

John Lewis raised his hand. "I move that we grant all those present permission to speak." The vote passed.

"Thank you, John, that will make the meeting less cumbersome," Sadie said. "Rev. Hawkins, the floor is yours."

Her heart pounded, her breathing was shallow and her mouth dry. Suzanne knew this was anxiety, but there was no help for it. She preferred to work out situations in a low key, subtle way in order to avoid polarization. It seemed to her that a person who is confronted tends to take a hard line, and then it becomes more difficult to communicate from then on. Or maybe that's a rationalization and I'm just a wimp like Bell thinks. She touched the cross Julie and Peter had given her and noticed that Peter was looking at the ceiling, their own private sign that said, "There's a dove flying about over your head."

Suzanne stood up and looked at each person. "I have thought hard about what to say today. This is, of course, very uncomfortable. No, it's more than uncomfortable. Such lies can damage a person's reputation. There is no truth to rumors that I am in any way unfaithful to my husband. If you can tell me why someone would spread rumors about me, that's what I'd like to know. Why has someone tried to hurt me? Why hurt the church?" She felt her anger rise, but was determined to present quiet confidence even though she was feeling far from quiet and not at all confident.

She looked around. JJ and Liz sat together and smiled at her. Bell gave her a surreptitious thumb's up. Peter sat on the edge of his chair. Julie looked pale. Then Tommy walked in, stiffly leaning on his cane and Mildred leaning on him. He shrugged her off and sat behind everyone. Suzanne knew it would be fruitless to suggest he and Mildred move up to the table. And then Morgan and Ralph entered the room and sat close to Sadie. All eyes went to Morgan. The caftan she wore didn't conceal that she was seven months pregnant. Is this intentional? Suzanne wondered. Ralph said they would take the attention away from me. Did he know about rumors back when we went to the prairie burn?

She cleared her throat and took a sip of water. "My inclination is to ignore rumors, but Sadie convinced me that talking with you all about them has a better chance of stopping them and also might contribute to our understanding of previous problems your church has had."

Sadie recognized one after the other who wanted to speak.

Bronwen was first. "This has nothing to do with previous problems."

"It has everything to do with them," Morgan said, arms around her unborn child.

Anna broke in, "Remember the rumors about Rev. Terry and money disappearing. There was no truth to it. I was on the committee that investigated. It was purely rumor. And there have been rumors about other people—untrue ones. It seems to me that there's an unholy hunger in this church for destructive rumors."

"That's not what the problem is," Tommy said. "This church managed fine until the presbytery started interfering."

Nobody picked up on that and the conversation took a turn.

"What does the Bible say?" one man asked, his double chin sitting on his chest just above his folded arms.

"About what?" Sadie asked him.

"About, you know, that homo stuff."

Bronwen answered, "The Bible says it's a sin. I think that's plain to see. It's against God's laws. I would never let a child of mine—."

Sadie broke in, "I'm sure that around this table we have varying opinions on that. And it would be a worthy subject for a class, but tonight we're dealing with rumors and the effect of them on your pastor and congregation. Any discussion about homosexuality needs to happen at a different time," Sadie said.

"Then what are we here to talk about?" Tommy said. "These rumors will hurt our church. You have to get rid of any suspicions."

"How do we go about getting a real pastor?" Mildred asked.

Suzanne's head jerked up.

Before Sadie could break in, Tommy said, "Is the presbytery going to keep us from having trustees again?"

"I can see that it is difficult to know what is appropriate to discuss," Sadie said. "After we conclude the purpose of this meeting, I will answer your questions about how a congregation chooses a pastor and decides whether they will have deacons and trustees in addition to elders.

"This meeting has one purpose, to bring recent rumors into the open so we can discuss how rumors start, how destructive they can be, and what we can do about them. It didn't occur to me that anyone would believe them. Does anyone have reason to believe the rumors?"

"How are we supposed to know? People say that where there's smoke there's fire," the man with the chins said. "I don't have any reason to believe the rumors or not to believe them. But if people think our pastor is fooling around or is 'one of those kind,' we're going to lose members, and we can't afford to lose members. I think it's time to get another pastor."

This is way out of hand, Suzanne thought. I should never have agreed to this.

Sadie looked him in the eye. "It is up to each of you to counteract gossip with the truth. I don't believe there is any truth to these rumors. If you think there is, then contact me and I'll tell you how to proceed."

"How do we know they're not true?" the man asked.

"There is no basis for this," Morgan said. "Someone made it all up out of thin air."

JJ stood up. "Madame Moderator, I'd like to say something." He took a deep breath. His hands shook. He clasped them behind his back. "It isn't enough to be pure. One has to look pure, too. We second-guess each other all the time. It seems to me we should ask questions and seek the truth instead of guessing." He paused. "I want to tell you the truth."

Bell sat up straight and his eyes got wide. Peter and Julie looked frightened. The rustling among the people at the tables stopped and all was quiet.

# CHAPTER 29

"Pastor Suzanne and I often have lunch together. That's no secret. I look forward to our talks. We discuss the scriptures she's going to preach on. Occasionally, I offer an illustration. We've become good friends. But I assure you there is no impropriety. I'm so sorry that this has grown into an embarrassment for our pastor. We haven't tried to keep these lunches secret. That should be a first clue that they are harmless.

"I think it's good we can talk this out together. Secrets are harmful." JJ said. "They can be destructive. They don't protect anyone. They just prolong confusion. I want to tell you a secret I've kept all my life. It will, I hope, confirm the truth about this situation.

"I've known since I was a little kid that I am gay. I never told anyone because I didn't want to hurt my parents, particularly my mother. I thought it would kill her. And I thought my dad would disown me. I didn't know anyone who was like me. Shoot, I didn't even know what to call it. Nobody talked about such things when I was growing up. When I did realize that some people like me had partners, I made the choice not to—again to protect my parents and to some degree to protect their business. So I have lived without a loving relationship in my life. It's lonely without companionship. I'd love to have a home life and children like other people.

"Anyway, Mother and Dad are gone now. It's time I told somebody. I don't want our pastor to be tainted by lies. She's been nothing but good to me, a true friend, and an excellent pastor. She helps me understand scripture and how to read the Bible with understanding. I – I guess that's all I have to say. It's your choice to accept me as I am or not." He sat down and wiped his eyes.

Suzanne looked down at the table. She hadn't known. What a loving sacrifice he had made for her. She tried to blink away tears but one fell on her hand. No one was looking at her though.

Sadie broke the long silence. "JJ, thank you. The truth will set us all free. Let's take a short break. Coffee and cookies are in the kitchen. When we come back, be ready to talk about why rumors start, what someone gets out of telling them, and what we can do to counteract them."

Liz hugged JJ, and others reassured him of their love. Beautiful, Suzanne thought. Julie and Peter gave her big hugs and she noticed Bell heading for Tommy. Suzanne watched to see if it was an angry confrontation, but Bell pulled out his wallet to show him a picture of the biggest fish he'd caught at the cabin. He's disarming him with all the charm he can muster, she thought. He can be a backslapping good old boy with the best of them.

Suzanne asked Julie to get her another glass of water and Peter to get their things into the car so they could leave as soon as the meeting was over.

It went on for another hour. Sadie brilliantly led them into a discussion of "good gossip" and "harmful gossip." "In the church we talk about each other all the time. When it's in loving concern it's good gossip. When it's hurtful, it's harmful gossip. It may at times be easy to slip into the harmful kind without intending to by telling others what we think we know even if it we have no way to know if it's true. Even if it's true, it can be hurtful to tell what someone doesn't want told.

"Tonight we're talking about intentionally starting rumors that are malicious. I'd like to open the floor for discussion about why someone would do this. What do you think?"

The responses came fast: "meanness," "spitefulness," "jealousy," "to seem important," "for attention," "for power," "to get rid of a pastor."

Peter spoke up. "Someone might have a big imagination and not be able to tell what's truth and what isn't."

Julie cringed as she always did when he spoke up in public.

Sadie wrote all the responses on newsprint. Then she said, "Good. If you think of some more reasons, we can put them up there, but let's move on now to discuss how you can know if someone is telling the truth or not. Ideas?"

Responses were slow to come on that question, but Liz finally got the discussion going. "A person gives wrong information regularly."

John Lewis added, "I am suspicious of sensational stories, ones that seem designed to get attention."

"Sometimes people tell me things that I know they can't have any way of knowing," Morgan said.

Most people looked interested and intent on the exchange of ideas, but Bronwen kept looking down, not engaging anyone in eye contact. Tommy sat with his cane between his legs, leaning back with his eyes closed.

Jewell Edwards had been quiet, but she looked around the table at each person intently, and then spoke up. "I ask how they know what they're telling me. It doesn't take long before nobody tells me anything."

There was a polite giggle.

"Doesn't the Bible tell us what to do if we have a quarrel with someone?" Ed Edwards as usual showed wisdom. "I think it says not to go around talking about it but to go directly to the person."

"Yes," Sadie said. "What else does it say?"

"As I recall, it says if you get no satisfaction, take two elders with you to talk with the person, and if there is still a problem, talk with the church, which I guess for us would be the Session. This would keep gossip down and people would deal with problems in such a way that they could be resolved."

"Thank you, Ed," Sadie sasid. "I know of no better way to wrap up this meeting. We've reviewed the harm that can come from rumors and gossip. We've ended up with some guidelines for how to respond to someone who brings us information." She pointed to the newsprint.

> *Challenge or ignore habitual misinformation*
> *Be suspicious of the truth of sensational stories*
> *Ask how they know what they're telling*
> *Ask why they're telling you*
> *Suggest they take the issue to the person involved*
> *If necessary, take elders with you*
> *Take it to the Session if none of the above resolve it.*

"As Presbyterians, you know we try to do things decently and in order. If you come across a problem that the Session cannot solve, they can go to the Committee on Ministry of the Presbytery for assistance. There is a whole process of charging a minister, elder or deacon with acting against their ordination vows. It is a process that treats the accused with fairness and the accuser with an avenue to pursue their charge. But that's enough about that for now. If you have any questions about how to proceed with something like that, you can always call me for clarification about the process. Rev. Bell Hawkins, will you close this meeting with prayer?"

Bell offered one of his famous, I'm-tired-and-let's-go-home prayers. "Lord, help us all to be your true people, loving you and loving each other. Amen."

Tommy and Mildred hung around and monopolized Sadie with

their questions. Tommy's harsh comments in the meeting didn't surprise Suzanne, but Mildred's did. *She wants to get rid of me? I thought she liked me. Maybe she was asking for Tommy. How will I respond to her when she comes to the church tomorrow?*

People chatted in two's and three's, but JJ hurried out after Suzanne gave him a big hug and a thank you. Liz and Morgan kept Suzanne busy debriefing the meeting. Bell took Julie and went on home, but Peter waited to ride with her. Finally they were in the car on the way home in the blessedly quiet night.

* * *

The silence held until they turned onto the turnpike. "Mom, that was awesome! People really talked to each other. They said good things, mostly. Of course that one man is always grouchy. And I don't know why that woman who's always at the church talked about a real pastor. She ought to know you're a real pastor. But I like the way people treated your friend JJ. And he was awesome. He told everybody that he's gay so they'd know you weren't. I like it when people talk to each other instead of guessing what everyone is thinking."

"Yes, it's awesome," Suzanne said.

"It was kinda like that thing you taught our youth group. You know, about solving a problem together. People said what they were thinking, and we ended up with a list of some things we can do to stop rumors."

Yes, she thought, although some of them moved right up there to a higher level when they jumped to the idea of getting rid of the pastor to solve the problem.

The tires kept a monotonous rhythm. Above the rolling flint hills of the prairie, the sky held a sliver of a moon and millions of stars. Peter fell asleep and made his sweet sleeping noises, reminding her of him as a baby. He would sleep soundly even if the telephone or doorbell rang or a pan dropped in the kitchen.

Her friends marveled and envied her. They had to get up several times a night with their babies.

"You don't deserve an easy baby," her mother had said. "You didn't sleep through the night until you were thirteen months old."

Peter hadn't been so easy since they moved to Kansas. Maybe she had kept him too close to her. She knew he had to break away, but it hurt. It hurt a lot when he barked at her and defied her. Bell insisted that she needed to back off and let him handle Peter in regard to his hair, earring, and tattoo. She still couldn't believe a child of hers had a tattoo. And his hair had been long ever since they moved, a gesture of defiance, she guessed. Lately he had begun wearing it in a ponytail instead of long and stringy. She thought Robert had something to do with Peter's more clean-cut look. Peter clearly admired Robert and wanted to be like him.

However, his latest look had come after doing a project for history class about the Lakota Native Americans. His class had taken a field trip to Lawrence where he interviewed students at Haskell Indian College. He came home from that enthralled with their stories. "All these different tribes go to school together and it's free."

Soon after that he dyed his hair black and began wearing one long braid. His chin and cheek bones had begun developing sharp angles, and he could pass for Indian. Mildred had asked him if he had Sioux blood. Of course, she did. Suzanne had fair skin and blond hair while Bell had graying brown hair. And neither of them had the beautiful bone structure of some American Indians.

Suzanne turned onto the road to Salina and let her mind wander. She still worried about splitting their family between two churches. They tried to attend major events at both, but that didn't really make them part of the family at Bell's or Bell part of the family at Covenant Church. The move to Kansas had put a strain on the family, or maybe all families had some kind of growing pains as children grew older. Julie still cuddled with both her parents and wanted to be tucked in at night. Such a sweet child, Suzanne thought. They both are, at heart.

There were still times when the bond she cherished with Peter showed up, usually when they were alone like tonight. As though he could hear her thinking, he awoke abruptly. "Mom, who do you think started those rumors?"

"I don't know. I find myself wondering, but then I start imagining it's this one and that one. It makes me suspicious of every person I talk to so I've decided that guessing hurts all my relationships in the church."

"You know, Mom, that meeting could change someone's life. It could change the whole church, too. It was so awesome, the way they came up with what to do," he whispered. "I think I want to be a pastor."

# CHAPTER 30

S UZANNE put the idea of leaving in the back of her mind until she could see the results of the meeting Sadie led. She said to Suzanne afterwards, "I told some of them that you don't need them. You can leave any time you want to, but they'll be left with themselves and their perennial problems."

Weeks later Liz said to Suzanne, "It's been nearly a month since the meeting. No rumors have popped up since then. At least I haven't heard anything. Nobody's even talking about Morgan as far as I've heard. Of course everybody knows I'm her Matron of Honor so they wouldn't say anything to me, I guess. You know, she's let her wedding dress out twice already, and she may need to do it again. I'm thinking twins or triplets, but she doesn't think so."

"Twins?" Mildred said, coming in the door.

We need to be more careful what we talk about in the office, Suzanne thought. She's always popping up when I don't even know she's in the building. She had come to the church nearly every day since the meeting about rumors and acted as if nothing had happened. One day she had pranced into Suzanne's office and in her sweet voice said, "I've been wondering what to do about Morgan. The women always throw a shower for a wedding and for a first baby. Which should we do first or should we do both at once? Or maybe we shouldn't do either. I heard she was pregnant before she and Ralph became an item."

183

"Where did you hear that?" Suzanne asked quickly.

"I don't remember. Anyway, I thought everyone knew."

"Just ask Morgan if she wants both at the same time or different times."

"Well," she said looking up at the ceiling, "I know you wouldn't marry them if –."

Suzanne interrupted her. "We don't need to have this conversation. The Session has approved the wedding and the baptism of the child."

"I guess it doesn't make any difference, but people are wondering."

"Wondering what? If people have questions or problems, please tell them to come and see me like we agreed you would. Mildred, it will be a big help to me if you will do that. And it could change this church for the good if people will start getting information instead of imagining or assuming."

"Okay," Mildred said as she held up her hands and tiptoed out backwards. "Whatever you say."

# CHAPTER 31

SUZANNE watched Morgan walking down the aisle toward her, toward Ralph. Her dark brown hair which she usually wore in a braid, today hung down past her shoulders in smooth waves held back by a simple headband made of lilies of the valley. She had grown them herself. More of the delicate white flowers along with yellow daffodils formed a bouquet. Clouds of tulle covered the floor length satin skirt. Liz and Morgan had embroidered tiny rosebuds into the skirt and train. There must have been a hoop under the skirt because it sat firmly across most of the aisle, barely leaving room for her uncle to escort her. The long train stretched out behind them.

Liz stood to Suzanne's right. Ralph and his brother stood on the left. The handsome groom occasionally wiped a tear off his cheek. The joy on his face and Morgan's repeated itself in the faces of friends, family, and church members who stood and followed with their eyes as this woman walked toward her future.

Suzanne had never heard a couple say "for better, for worse" with as much feeling.

As far as she knew only she and Liz and, of course, Ralph were aware that the baby was conceived as a result of a rape. Morgan insisted that she had come to terms with it and intended to claim the baby as hers and Ralph's. "The baby is a blessing," she said often. Ralph wouldn't say much when they talked about it during the wedding counseling sessions. And so Suzanne respected their wishes even though she remained alert in case the truth reared its ugly head and the young couple needed to deal with it further.

"The women teased Morgan about what health foods she had put in the cake," Liz told Suzanne the next day. "She told them 'sauerkraut' just to give them something to talk about. I've never seen the women of this church so giddy. You know, we don't have many weddings. And it's been a long time since we had a baby, too."

"It looked to me like every one came to the wedding and the wedding shower," Suzanne said.

"Yes, anyone not there was accounted for. I'm so glad nobody boycotted it. I think they'll all come to the baby shower, too. Since we're waiting until after the baby comes, everyone will want to come and hold it. Maybe it's too early to say, but I think there is a definite shift in attitude in the church. My grandmother said that she could remember a time when a pregnant woman would have been denied a wedding in the church.

# CHAPTER 32

CHURCH activities usually slowed down after school let out and people left for vacations. But June kept a steady pace.

The always-frantic Vacation Bible School week followed the wedding. "Thirty-five children, that's more than last year," Liz said, "I love seeing all the little ones having fun and learning, but my, isn't it loud?

"It is," Suzanne said. "But the first day is always the most hectic while everyone figures out what to expect. They sure sang with gusto this morning. I'm glad so many youth group members came to help."

By Friday, Suzanne felt anxious. Not only did Bible School take away her day off, she also had no sermon ready for Sunday so she would miss any time with the family on Saturday, too. She helped clean up after all the children left Friday afternoon, and packed up her sermon notes to take home. But the phone rang, and she waited while Liz answered.

"Tommy Lewis has been taken to the hospital," Liz said. "Infected toe. It's serious. He has diabetes."

Suzanne sat down hard in her desk chair. Do I have to go? she asked herself.

Liz came in. "Don't do it," she said. "He'll just be mean to you again. It's not like he's dying."

"If I don't go, people will have more to talk about."

"You're so tired. Maybe it can wait until Sunday."

"If I don't go now, I'll worry about it, and what if it is really serious, like what if he dies? I'd feel really bad then. So, I'll go by there and at least pop in and have a prayer with him on my way home."

* * *

As she approached his room, she heard his booming voice. "Get me some water and another blanket. And I need a bigger one of these. Get me a new one that covers up my backside."

When Suzanne entered the room, he grimaced. "I'm not dying."

"I expect it will take more than a sore toe to do you in," she grinned.

He looked away from her and never met her eyes the rest of the time she was there.

"Would you like to have a prayer?"

He shrugged.

Suzanne's inner imp mischievously showed up. "Lord, this man is in need of your help even if he won't admit it. Give him the wisdom to know what he needs and the grace to accept it from all who care for him. And give us all rest and peace, we pray. Amen"

"I'm on my way home. It's been a long week with VBS, and I still have a sermon to write for Sunday. Do you want me to come by and preach it for you Sunday afternoon?" She grinned.

"Hmmph," he said.

That was fun, she told herself as she got into her car. I think I've found a way to talk with him without getting so frustrated.

# CHAPTER 33

THE last two weeks of June, the youth group took a ten-day mission trip to Mexico. They planned to paint and do some construction. Suzanne's worries about Peter and Julie going so far away had lessened when Ed and Jewell explained to the parents that they had done this before and they knew the churches on the border where they would be working. Eight young people and four adults left in two vans with tools and supplies and lots of excitement.

Then the church became too quiet. Suzanne used the time to work ahead on sermons and to meditate. She had neglected her prayers and centering practices, and she needed to get back to them. It's also time to take stock of where we are and when is the best time to leave, she thought.

She began her days by taking her Bible and notebook into the dark sanctuary. The only light came from morning beams slanting through the stained glass. She immediately felt bathed in peace. In the past it had taken her several days of practice before that peace settled over her, but in the holy space of the third pew from the back she quickly fell into God's arms. Her mind stopped its clamoring and its insistent picking at bits of conversation and items on her to do list. She let it all go except her concern and constant prayers for the group in Mexico. God, keep our mission team safe. Show your love through them. Help Julie and Peter be wise and alert.

It didn't help her anxiety that her mother had called numerous times over the previous month. "Darlin', don't let those children go down there. It's dangerous. Didn't you hear about that boy who died last month when he was on vacation in Mexico?"

"Yes, Mother, I heard. He walked in front of a bus. That could happen anywhere."

"But, Suzanne Marie, these are your children. Please, don't let them go."

I will not be a nervous parent. I will not be overly protective. She had to talk herself into not falling into her mother's patterns of anxiety over every little thing. It had taken years and distance to be somewhat free of that anxiety and perfectionism. Her mother's voice still lived in her head, but she'd learned to talk back in her mind. Occasionally, she was even calm about it.

I keep my children safe, I teach them to be careful without hovering and correcting every little thing they do. I sure hope I never give Mother a reason to say, "I told you so."

\* \* \*

One day Liz interrupted her morning meditation. "Morgan's at the hospital! I've got to go coach her. At the last minute Ralph is too squeamish to be present at the birth. He says he'll pace in the waiting room like men are supposed to do."

Suzanne went to be with him, and he did indeed pace. Beads of sweat covered his pale face. Finally, a nurse directed them to wash their hands thoroughly and put on masks and gowns. In the birthing room, Ralph was handed a little girl and then another little girl. He looked like he was going to drop them or drop to the floor himself. So Suzanne got to hold one of them and Liz the other for a few seconds before the nurse placed them back on their mother's chest. Morgan beamed and then winced. "Woo, it's not over, I guess."

The nurse laughed, "It's not another baby. These contractions will expel the placenta."

Liz moved to Morgan's side to hold her hand, and Suzanne led Ralph back to the waiting room where she got a cold cloth for his head. "Have you picked out names, Ralph?" she asked him.

"Names? No, we've talked, but um, uh."

"Plenty of time," she told him.

Five days later Morgan went home but had to leave the babies in the hospital for a while longer. "It's excruciating, Suzanne, excruciating. I just want to get them here at home so I can be sure they're all right. And I can hold little Julia and Miriam."

I won't rest until my babies are back in the nest, too, Suzanne thought as she hung up.

The phone rang again. Liz took the call, and from her end of the conversation, Suzanne could tell something was wrong. She moved to the doorway between their offices and saw Liz rummaging through her desk drawer as she talked.

"What is it?" Suzanne asked.

"Tornado. Grandmother and Buddy will be here any minute. We've got to get the emergency supplies and go to the basement. We're an emergency shelter so we leave the door unlocked and put this outside. She handed Suzanne a magnetic sign."

"Take the key to Mildred's room. We'll use it if she doesn't come." Suzanne called over her shoulder as she ran to put the sign on the metal door. "Shelter in Basement" it proclaimed in red.

By the time they had gathered the shopping bags of supplies from Liz's closet, Buddy and Anna blew through the door. "Come on, Buddy Boy." Anna pulled him away from looking at the sky. There was no sign of Mildred or anyone else in the parking lot.

"To the basement," Liz shouted. She handed Buddy a portable radio to carry, one shopping bag to her grandmother, another to Suzanne, and she carried a stack of blankets down the stairs.

"I hope this key works," Liz said to Suzanne, handing her the blankets. "I never actually tried it." She had to jiggle it and pull on the door to get it to unlock, but finally they were in the little parlor-like room.

Suzanne brought two more chairs in from the fellowship hall while Liz tried to get reception on the radio. Finally, she set it outside the door of the room and the local station came in clearly.

*A line of thunderstorms is approaching the city of Middletown. We've received reports of tornadoes in central Colorado and western Kansas. This just in from our crews on the ground: A tornado has been spotted west of Middletown and moving east. All residents of Middletown and those living directly west of town are advised to take cover now. I repeat, go to your safe place, an interior room or basement. Stay away from windows. Take cover now.*

Anna sat down in one of the pulpit chairs with Buddy beside her, snuggled under her arm. She opened a photograph album to show him pictures. "Look at how these people are dressed, Buddy," she said.

But he looked around the room. "What is this place?" he asked.

"It's Mrs. Olsen's history room," his mother told him as she sat down in a folding chair beside him. "See up there. Those are pictures of the old churches and our pastors through the years."

"Where's that one?" he asked pointing to the empty spot in the row.

"That's where Rev. Terry belongs. Nobody can find his picture. It went missing and it's a mystery where it is," Liz said.

At the word 'mystery' his little blond head jerked up, and he left his grandmother's chair to look around.

Liz kept checking the radio station. She had to leave the door open so she could hear the reports. That gave them air, too. "If we hear a tornado coming, I'll shut the door," she said. "Grandmother, will you be sure Buddy's under that table with a blanket over him. I'll lie down on top of him, and you two should cover your heads with blankets." She threw each of them a blanket and then unpacked the shopping bags, placing items in the big closet where Mildred kept the silver. A jar of water, a canteen, paper cups, candy bars, flashlights, a first aid kit, a siren. Suzanne started to ask about the siren and then realized that they could be buried if the building above them fell. Maybe nobody would be able to find them. "I'm putting anything in here that might fly around," Liz said. "We'll close this door, too."

Suzanne began shaking. Where in Mexico are Julie and Peter right now? Where is Bell? Do they know about this tornado? What if we die in here? Will anybody ever find us? What else should we do to be safe? Suzanne felt her chest tighten and her breaths come short and shallow. She had to go to the bathroom.

Buddy distracted her. "Look what I found?" He held up a picture.

Anna took it from him. "It's Rev. Terry. Where did you find it?"

"Grandmama, it was behind that," he said, pointing to the metal cabinet in the closet. He crawled over to show her how he reached around the back near the floor. "I see something else back there." He stretched his arm out and reached as far as he could, his eyes closed and face wrinkled up in concentration. "No," he said, "it's just a bug."

He kept looking around feeling under the cabinet and surprised them by finding something else. He pulled out a key from under a corner of the cabinet with a little yelp of triumph. "What do you think it's to?" he asked and took it to continue his explorations.

Liz hung the picture in its place on the wall and then quickly darted to the radio to listen to the latest warning details. Suzanne arranged the blankets half folded and placed them to be accessible. Anna placed candy bars, flashlights and the canteen of water under the table.

"Grandmama, I found something else." Buddy said, handing a thin photograph album to Anna. "I saw it under a shelf. It was taped up there where nobody could see it. Do you think it's been there a long time? Maybe it's a buried treasure map."

The lights went out, and Suzanne handed each one a flashlight. Liz reported that the crew on the ground had radioed in to the station that a tornado was on the ground north of town. Anna spread a blanket on the floor under the table and laid another beside it. Buddy and Liz sat there under the table while Suzanne and Anna threw blankets around their shoulders.

In one hand Liz held a flashlight and in the other the album Buddy had found. She hefted it as though trying to decide by its weight whether to open it. In one swift move, Buddy took it and opened it up. "It's just pictures," he said and handed it back to his grandmother.

Liz scurried back to open the door and listen to the radio. "Tornadoes south of us now," she reported. "I can hear the rain. Quite a thunderstorm."

They sat, as though around a campfire, Anna looking through the photos, exclaiming, gasping, mumbling. Finally, she said, "This is very disturbing. Suzanne, remember the picture of you and JJ in the paper, the one of you wearing the hat and shawl?"

"Yes."

"That picture is in here but your face has been covered up by a photo of Mildred's face. And that's the most recent of many similar ones. There is a picture of her as a child pasted onto a scene of children playing in a park and another of her on the porch of the house I grew up in. This is bizarre."

She kept turning pages. "Here's a high school picture of several of us out in a boat. Tommy's rowing. She wasn't really there, but she's put herself in the boat."

"She's mentioned more than once Tommy singing to her in a boat out on the lake," Liz said.

Buddy fell asleep and Liz covered him up. "He's quite the little investigator," she said.

Suzanne took the album and thumbed through it. "What do you think this is all about?"

Anna shook her head. Her white hair looked silver in the glow of her flashlight. "This is so sad. I had no idea her pain went so deep and persisted all this time. She grew up poor, a pitiful child, nose always running, clothes dirty and often torn. She smelled bad, and no one wanted to be near her. None of us took pity on her. We didn't know, couldn't comprehend her life. We were so wrapped up in ourselves.

"Her father was the town drunk. We didn't even know the word, "alcoholism," never thought of him having a disease. This is seventy years ago, you know. The kids made fun of her mother. She was the janitor at our elementary school and she had wild hair. It was black and stuck out all over. We called her the wild woman of Borneo. My, my, we were cruel.

"In high school Mildred had a few friends. She came to school clean. I think the school nurse helped her."

"Was that when she and Tommy dated?" Suzanne asked.

"Tommy? They were never an item. She would've liked that. We were all googoo eyed over him. He was tall and handsome, a football star. Most of us admired him from afar, but Mildred thrust herself at him, dressing provocatively—which in that time meant skirts above the ankle. Hers rose steadily. The first I ever saw of the scandalous roaring twenties style was on her, skirts nearly to the knee. What a tart! And she had a red hat I remember that we all envied. I don't know where she got the money for clothes like that."

Liz got up to check the radio. "Nothing new. When did her husband come into the picture?"

"Hmmm, let's see. Fred went to high school nearby. I can't think which little town it was. They married a couple of years after we graduated. Mildred had come into disfavor with the people in town because she told some girls she was pregnant by Tommy. The whispers got around town, and when Tommy's parents heard them, they were mortified. Those o-so-proper Lewises lost favor in the Welsh community. In that time such shame followed a person to the grave. Tommy quickly went off to join the Army Air Corps.

"It all blew over when Mildred didn't 'blossom' as they said back then. People avoided saying the word 'pregnant.' There was still some taint on the family from the rumors until Tommy came back in his uniform, all decorated, and hailed a hero. Mildred's reputation, well, let's just say, it never was stellar and it went downhill after that. But that was so long ago, very few would remember it now.

"Even so, she's part of the family. And the family takes care of its own. When Mildred and Fred's house burned down, Tommy came to their aid as he has with so many."

The radio squawked and squealed. Liz opened the door. "It's coming right at us," the announcer said. "Take shelter. Take shelter now!" And the radio went silent.

Liz closed the door and the closet and threw herself over Buddy. Anna and Suzanne covered their heads with blankets. Thunder boomed. The storm rumbled. Above their heads a crash. The chancel is above us, Suzanne thought. Was that the brass candlesticks? She held the siren in case they were buried and needed to get attention. There was more crashing overhead. Buddy sobbed. Liz soothed. A low rumble got closer, a crescendo, a roar. Her ears hurt. The ceiling sounded like it was coming down on them.

"Lord, help us," Suzanne prayed with each breath. "The Lord is my shepherd."

Silence. Waiting.

Anna said, "I think it's over. Is everyone okay?"

Suzanne carefully opened the door. The radio produced only

static. "Well, at least we can get out the door," she said. "I'll go check on things."

* * *

Damage to the church included a broken stained glass window, two huge trees uprooted in the front yard, and roof damage. Limbs and several different kinds of shingles covered the ground. The rest of the neighborhood was similarly affected. A trailer park north of town had been flattened. A woman and her baby died after being thrown from their trailer by the wind.

Since they had no electricity and no phone, Liz took Anna and Buddy to check on their house. When she returned, she reported to Suzanne that her house survived with minimal damage, just a few shingles blown off. She had phone service so she had called the police station and the Red Cross to let them know the church was open for any who needed a place to stay though the electricity was stll off. She also had called Morgan who reported that they had gone to her store to take cover and were back at home. Their trailer was untouched. Also Morgan was collecting food and bringing it to the church in case people took shelter there. Liz took inventory of their supplies for sheltering in preparation for conferring with the Red Cross about what help was needed.

While she did that, Suzanne drove to Mildred's. Liz was worried about her since she always came to the church during a tornado outbreak.

Mildred opened the door. Her hair was tousled, she was barefoot. She didn't invite Suzanne in, but as Liz had told her, Mildred's house was quite a sight. Tall stacks of newspapers and magazines sat next to the couch and along the wall wherever there was space. The coffee table held several cups and saucers, glasses, a bottle of wine, boxes of crackers and dried out chunks of cheese. The rank musk of mildew wafted out of the house.

Suzanne held the rogue photo album in plain sight. "Are you okay?" she asked. "We were worried about you."

"I'm okay. I was taking a nap, but when I woke with the thunder it was too late to leave the house. I've been calling all the members to see if they're okay. So far nothing to report."

"Well, good. The phone is out at the church so I'm glad you're making calls. This is yours," she said handing her the album. "Better keep it here."

She took it without comment, without a look of shame and without a smile or word of gratitude. Nor did she ask how she had entered "her history room."

"I'll be at the church waiting in case anyone comes there. Do you need anything?"

Mildred shook her head and closed the door before Suzanne had fully turned around to leave.

# CHAPTER 34

THE day the youth group returned, parents and friends lined the church driveway cheering and waving signs and balloons. When the travelers unfolded themselves from the vehicles and blinked their eyes, friends and family members hugged them. Suzanne remembered how disoriented she had felt when returning home from her first mission trip.

Peter and Julie looked taller. They looked older. And they looked tired.

They drove home in silence. The two travelers slept, but then they talked all during dinner.

"The children begged us for coins or food or anything," Julie said. "I didn't know what to do. They were so little and wore just rags, no shoes. Mrs. Edwards said not to give them anything right then, we'd give them all we could before we left.

"I read to them—all the children's books Mrs. Edwards took," Julie said. "When we left, she gave them the books. Their little eyes... so happy..." Julie teared up and Peter took over.

"We built a ramp for a woman in a wheelchair. We made a playground for the children out of old tires, and we painted a whole house. Mr. Edwards showed us how to do everything."

"And we repaired a porch, too," Julie added.

"I'm really proud of you two," Bell said. He beamed at his children. "You know, it was awfully quiet around here except for a tor-nado."

* * *

They settled into a summer routine in July. Julie and Peter went to work with Suzanne where they found plenty to do. With Matthew and Sarah they formed a playgroup for children five to ten years old and even earned some money when parents found out what good babysitters they were. They took the group to free movies, played games at the park and one day taught them some simple origami. They also faithfully tutored at the church, reading books for fun, now that there were no school assignments. The program kept expanding, even including some parents who wanted to learn to read English.

Suzanne and Bell used a few vacation days for their family to join the Edwards family at the lake. And one hot and steamy day, Suzanne and Bell helped chaperone their combined church youth groups on a trip to Worlds of Fun in Kansas City.

In August Suzanne set about taking stock of the health of the congregation. She hadn't yet decided about the right moment to leave. The twins' baptism was coming up. Maybe, she thought, the more time that passes, the easier it will be to see clearly the source of the congregation's dysfunction. She still hoped to leave them better off than when she arrived. Besides all that, they weren't anywhere close to ready to call another pastor. There was still much work to be done. They might be able to call another interim, but as far as she knew, there was no one in the presbytery who was available for that.

She sat in the sanctuary in the morning light, thinking, doodling, and making notes. The rumors about her had stopped, as far as she knew. She and JJ still met for lunch but invited anyone in the congregation to join them to discuss the next Sunday's scriptures. Anna and Mildred often were there along with one or two others.

The mood of the congregation had lifted with the wedding and then again when the twins were born. Sundays, both men and women positioned themselves in a line to hold little Miriam and Julia.

The levels of conflict had been referred to several times in session meetings when some little decision began to grow horns. The list sat before them on newsprint at every meeting. That seemed to be helping, so far.

What else? Relationships—she'd seen no rifts, although past resentments still hovered in the air. Worship attendance—slightly better than when she started with them. The tutoring project and the mission trip showed some positive energy outside themselves. Sunday school, choirs, and the youth group all held steady and overall had doubled in numbers. They were excellent programs. That was a sign of good and active leadership; although, as usual, only twenty per cent of the people did the work. Complaints were few though that wasn't surprising in the summertime. It might change in the fall when regular programs began again. Finances were holding steady, always just enough to cover the bills. But when the roof needed repairs, people had come out of the woodwork to pitch in for that.

Of course, Tommy still thought trustees would solve all the problems. His financial support of the congregation could hold them hostage to his desires if he decided to press his will on an issue. So far he hadn't, and the Session had begun making decisions without verbalizing the desire to please him.

Mildred did continue to point out what he'd like or be unhappy with. Suzanne wondered if she alone could be the source of all the discontent. She continued to exert her influence by gathering knowledge and sharing it freely, even if it wasn't always accurate, but Liz said everyone knew to take whatever she said with a grain of salt.

# CHAPTER 35

Tommy entered the hospital again. The infection in his toe had spread. Suzanne visited regularly, but he rarely looked at her or said anything. One day, in an attempt to get some response, she asked if his big toe had gone to market and his little one wee wee weed all the way home, but she succeeded in entertaining only herself. She prayed, "Lord, let your grace fall upon this man. Let your compassion free him from pain and despair." He said not a word.

As she got up to leave, Liz barged into his room.

"Peter—tree limb, hit his head, ER." She grabbed Suzanne's arm and they ran down the hall, taking the steps instead of the elevator.

Her heart was pounding, and she was out of breath when they reached the nurse's station. "My son, Peter Hawkins," she said.

"Right this way. You'll need to wait out here while they get him cleaned up and the doctor examines him, but you can look in from the edge of the curtain."

Blood covered his head and the sheet. She couldn't see his eyes. Oh, no, oh, no. God no. He's got to be okay.

"Bell," Suzanne cried over the phone at the nurses' station. "There's been an accident. Peter's hurt. A tree limb fell on him. I don't know how bad it is. We're at the hospital, but I can't go in to see him yet."

"I'm on my way," he said. "I'll get there as quickly as I can." She handed the phone to the nurse and hurried back to the cubicle.

Liz tapped her on the shoulder. "Suzanne, Robert's here," she whispered.

They stepped back into a hallway. "Robert, what happened?"

He had blood on him, too, and his eyes looked glazed. "A big limb fell on his head. No wind, no warning. He and Matt were throwing the Frisbee while I went in the library for a minute. When I came out, I heard the crack. No time to warn him. I keep wondering though if I had could have screamed or run to him quicker. . ."

"Was he unconscious?" Suzanne asked.

"At first, yes, but I don't know after the ambulance came."

Liz put her arm around him. "Come with me. You're in shock. Let's get a nurse to see you, too."

Then Matt was there. "Is he okay? Is he going to be okay? He has to be. He's my best friend. I don't know why this would happen to him. He's such a good person."

Sarah and Julie followed Matt into the hallway and hugged Suzanne. Wide-eyed, the three of them looked at her with questions in their eyes. "I don't know anything yet," Suzanne said. "I haven't talked to the doctor. Who else is here?"

"My family and Liz," Sarah answered.

Good, Suzanne thought. Jewell and Ed will take care of everybody.

"Julie, your dad will be here in about an hour—no, probably sooner. Watch for him and show him where I am. I'll come tell you when I know anything."

As soon as they left, she stepped back to the cubicle and from the edge of the curtain, she glued her eyes on Peter, unable to do anything but pray as a nurse gently dabbed at his face.

O God, please. Please.

She stopped a nurse. "Can you tell me anything? Can I go in yet?"

"We have him cleaned up now, and we're talking with two doctors, keeping them up to date. The on call doctor has already been in, and the other is a head trauma specialist at KUMed. Fortunately he's been in Salina today, so he'll be here soon."

"I need to go in and tell Peter I'm here."

The nurse hesitated. "Rev. Hawkins, he's still unconscious—."

"Unconscious?" The nurse grabbed both her arms and steadied her. "I didn't know. That's not good, is it?"

"Head injuries are all different. It will take a while to know how serious this is. You need to prepare yourself for a long wait. Meantime, you need to to maintain your strength and collect every bit of patience you can. We will keep you advised of even the slightest change. Do you have anyone with you?"

"Yes, they're in the waiting room, and my husband's on the way."

"Okay. I'll go in with you, but he needs minimal stimulation. Talk softly to your son, sing quietly to him if you want to, be strong and positive. He may hear you even though he doesn't respond."

She took a deep breath as the nurse opened the curtain. "Be prepared for lots of equipment monitoring him. Are you okay?"

Suzanne nodded. Okay? Okay? No, I'm not okay. My sweet boy is. . .

"Is there any chance that he won't, that he might not, um. . . ?" she whispered.

"The first twenty-four hours are very important," the nurse said leading the way in.

Peter lay in a bed raised high off the floor with railings on the sides to keep him from rolling out. Just like when he was a baby, she thought, except for the mask on his face and the IV in his arm. O God, please.

The nurse watched her like a hawk. She's waiting to see if I will faint, Suzanne thought. She stood taller. I can do this. Peter needs me to do this.

She held his hand, trying to ignore the beeps of equipment connected to him. "Peter, I'm here, sweetheart." He didn't move. His eyelids looked soft and vulnerable. "You've had an accident, and you're at the hospital. Robert and Matt took good care of getting you here. They're in the waiting room with Julie and Sarah. Your dad will be here soon. There are some good doctors and nurses taking care of you." She paused and quietly sang, "So high you can't get over it, so low you can't get under it, so wide you can't get around it. You must come in at the door." Tears started to form. She felt queasy.

The nurse brought in a chair, and she sat holding his hand, willing her life into him. O God, please, please. She talked to Peter, she sang, she stared at him, she rubbed his hand, she rested her head on the bed railing.

A nurse wearing a mask entered. "We're ready to take him to ICU. You can walk along with us most of the way."

"Peter, we're going to another room. I'll be close by all the time. Dad will be here soon." He lay there, still and silent.

I wish he'd sit up and argue with me. I'll never mention his hair, his earring, or his tattoo again. O God, please.

As they wheeled Peter out into the hall, Julie and Bell came rushing around the corner. Suzanne had hold of Peter's hand. Bell gave her a half hug and walked behind her, touching Peter's foot. "Dad's here and Julie," Suzanne said. Julie held onto her dad's arm.

At the elevator, they had to let go of him and trust the nurse to watch after their boy. "Julie, will you tell those in the waiting room that we're moving up to the ICU waiting room? Thank them and tell them we don't know anything. They can wait with us if they want, but we won't know anything for a long time. We will call them if they want to go on home."

"I got it, Mom. Peter, you wake up, you hear me?" she whispered. Her wavery voice belied her bossy tone.

The volunteer at the desk in the ICU waiting room recognized Suzanne and met her with a warm smile. "Pastor, who are you here to see?"

"It's my boy. A tree limb fell on him."

"Oh, no. Let's get you set up over in the alcove. We don't have many people today so you can have as much room as you need. As you know the coffee is over against the wall. Visits are limited to ten minutes beginning at ten before the hour and ten before the half hour. Only two people at a time. Let me know if you need anything."

The alcove provided the only semblance of privacy in the room. A low round table sat in the middle of two couches and three chairs. At the other end of the larger room past rows of empty chairs, a white-haired couple sat at a table near the coffee station working a jigsaw puzzle.

Suzanne didn't want to sit down. She wanted to see where they had taken Peter. "I'll be right back," she told Bell. She found the ICU. Through the windows in the double doors, she could see two of the cubicles. One had the curtain closed. In the other, nurses surrounded the bed checking monitors and lines and tubes. When one of them moved, she could see Peter's face turned toward her, his eyes still closed. She stood there frozen in place until Julie found her.

"Mom, I couldn't find you." Julie's voice broke. "I couldn't find you anywhere."

"I'm right here," Suzanne said and gave her a hug. "Look, you can see Peter through there."

When they returned to the waiting room, the alcove was nearly full. Ed and Bell stood together and nearby Jewell sat with Robert, Matt and Sarah. Liz hung up the phone at the volunteer's desk.

"Any change?" Jewell asked.

"No, no change. I'm hoping a doctor will tell us something soon." Suzanne sat down on a couch and Julie snuggled up next to her.

Bell communicated silently with raised eyebrows, and she shook her head.

"We're into the 'if only's,'" Bell said. "But I told them that there is no guilt here. Sometimes things just happen."

Suzanne nodded. "This is a freak accident. Nobody's fault."

"But why would this happen to Peter?" Matt asked. "Why him?"

Liz answered. "Suzanne, I remember your sermon about bad things happening to good people. You said, 'Don't ask "Why me?" ask "What now?"'"

The phone rang, and the volunteer talked a long time while everyone in the room stared at her and held their breath. But she hung up without communicating anything.

Other phone calls jerked them up and down, but no word came from the doctor.

A fruit basket arrived with a note from JJ. "I'm praying and holding you all in my heart."

Ed chuckled. "He doesn't come to the hospital for fear somebody will think he's come for them or their loved one. Or they'll think he's an ambulance-chasing funeral director. His father set that rule for them years ago. They only show up at the hospital when specifically asked to."

Mildred and Mary stirred the tense air when they popped in on their way upstairs to get Tommy and take him home. Mildred announced her entry with a "Yoohoo," and waved to everyone in the room, then tiptoed over to kiss Suzanne on the forehead. "We'll be back later," she said.

John and Bronwen arrived, and Bell repeated the same no news conversation they'd had with everyone. Then all settled down to wait. The adults sat in the alcove and the young people took over the jigsaw puzzle the older couple had abandoned.

Tommy came in pushed in a wheelchair by Mary. Mildred walked beside him, looking possessive with a hand on his arm.

"How's the boy?" he asked in a booming voice which didn't fit his folded over body.

The same words they'd said over and over, circled the room again. "No change." "Still unconscious." "Waiting to hear from the doctor."

Tommy got out of the wheelchair with the help of his cane and hobbled over to a chair close to the men. When he waved his hand, Mildred and Mary disappeared with the wheelchair. Good, Suzanne thought, the men will keep each other occupied for a while. Is Tommy here to collect more ammunition against me? He'll probably say a mother can't continue being a pastor in this circumstance. And he'd probably be right. This may well be the time to leave without having to explain why.

Suzanne and Bell went to see Peter at the first visiting opportunity. They stood beside his bed and murmured while holding his hands. He looked peaceful. "We're here, sweetheart," Suzanne said.

"We're always close by," Bell whispered in his ear.

On the way back to the waiting room, they saw Mildred and Mary in the hall carrying boxes of pizza. Robert trailed behind them. "You haven't had any lunch today," Mildred said. "Robert, put those drinks on the table and see if there is ice in the little refrigerator. You two take these. We've got to go, but we'll be back later."

"We should pray," Julie said when everyone had some food. She looked around and when she got to Robert, she stopped. "Robert, would you?"

He cleared his throat. "Let us pray: Loving and merciful God, join us together as only you can. Wrap your arms around Peter and around us. Bring him healing in whatever ways you choose. Give us faith, we pray, as we seek to trust in you this day. We thank you for this food that will nourish us in body as you keep us nourished in spirit. We pray in Jesus' name. Amen."

"Fine young man," Tommy said as Robert and the other young

people left for a spot across the room. "You've done a great job raising him," he said to Ed and Jewell. "Fine job."

"He's a very special person," Jewell said. "Ed and I can't take all the credit. I think he was born an old soul."

John chimed in, "He certainly is sensitive to other people's needs. Unusual for a person his age." Bronwen nodded and dipped her head.

"Today brings back painful memories," Jewell said to Suzanne. "We sat here a long, long time waiting for Rose to wake up."

Ed broke in. "But that was more severe than this," he said a little too quickly.

"Yes, of course," Jewell said. "But we know how hard it is to wait. We know how to do this."

That must be why these particular people are the ones to stay close by, Suzanne thought. They understand. But in the moment all that mattered was Peter. She would think about the rest later.

# CHAPTER 36

Liz took Julie home to get clothes and toiletries for all of them. Visitors came and went. Jewell took phone calls and explained that they didn't know much. Mildred called often and said that she was keeping the church people informed.

Each of Suzanne's sisters called, and her mother cried so hard on the phone she couldn't talk. After that, they appointed her sister Rebecca, a nurse, to be the communicator for the family. She said that any or all of them would come as soon as she gave the go ahead. Suzanne declined for now until she knew more, but she felt surrounded by much love.

She curled up on a couch and faced the corner. Needing to be alone, she wrapped herself in a blanket and covered her head with a white afghan Morgan had sent with Liz. Bell handled moments like this by talking, but she needed quiet, no more input, no more feeling. She withdrew into herself, into God's arms. She recalled napping with baby Peter, both of them in the fetal position. She had held him close to keep him safe from the world that would pull him away from her. Now she wanted to climb into his bed and hold him, and breathe life into him.

She jumped when the phone rang. Bell and the others stopped chattering. Long seconds went by as the volunteer talked in low tones and finally hung up.

"Mr. and Mrs. Hawkins, the doctor will see you in Consultation Room A."

She moved so quickly Bell had to help her get untangled from the blanket.

* * *

The little room held three chairs and a table with a telephone and a sign, "Call 001 if no one arrives in twenty minutes."

Ten long minutes went by, and finally the doctor appeared. Suzanne tried to read his face. His forehead was wrinkled, and as he talked, his eyes looked at them but not really at them. It was as though he were looking at the insides of his eyeballs. "Your son is very lucky," he said. "Another inch... well, let me tell you what we know." He gave so much detail Suzanne's own eyes began to glaze over.

When they returned to the waiting room, Liz was back and the children were hovering around the adults: Tommy, Bronwen and John, Ed and Jewell. They all looked up expectantly, and Bell summarized what they had learned. "He's still unconscious. The head wound needed stitches but the limb didn't penetrate the skull. That's very good news. There is no need for surgery. The CT scan shows no injury to the brain that they can see. He told us to be patient, that every head wound is different. He said we might see some movements but not to get too excited. Right now they will most likely be reactive not responsive. What we will look for long term is a response such as raising his hand if he's told to."

"Will he be okay?" Julie asked.

Bell put his arm around her shoulder. "He's going to live, but we won't know any long term effects for a while." He gave her a little hug. "It's twenty after. Want to go with me to visit Peter?"

Jewell said, "It's about time for you kids to go home. Suzanne, do you want Julie to stay with us?"

"I've got beds ready for anyone who wants to stay at our house," Bronwen said.

"Thanks, Bronwen. I think Julie will want to stay with Sarah, but Bell and I might take turns napping at your house."

"I'm going down to the chapel for a few minutes," Robert said, "and then I'll take the little squirts home."

When Matt and Sarah went back to the jigsaw puzzle, Suzanne noticed Jewell holding Bronwen's hand. The older woman's tears flowed freely. Tommy was on the phone, and Ed and John stood talking at the coffee pot.

Suzanne waited until Robert had taken his brother and sister and Julie home before she said what was on her heart to Bronwen, Jewell, their husbands and Tommy. "Bell and I are blessed to have you here. Thank you for being with us."

Ed spoke. "If we can do anything to help, well, speaking for myself, I'd do anything."

"I know this must be painful for you all to relive," Suzanne said.

Jewell took over. "We waited here, in this very room, hoping. But it only took a few hours before they told us to prepare ourselves. Bronwen and John's lovely girl. I could not believe that she would leave us. She was so full of life and light."

"God saw fit to take Rose," Tommy said wiping away a tear. "I hope he looks with more favor on your boy."

"I don't think God works like that," Bell said. "This was a freak accident."

"If the city had kept those trees trimmed, it wouldn't have happened." Tommy leaned forward, blood vessels in his large forehead pulsing. "I gave them an ear full and told them they'd better be ready to pay these hospital bills. When I was mayor, this wouldn't have happened."

"I don't think this is anybody's fault," Bell said.

"I won't blame anyone, and I don't think God causes things like this to happen, either."

"You don't believe in God's punishment?" Tommy asked.

"I think punishing is different from teaching," Bell answered.

Tommy closed his eyes and leaned back.

He's weary, Suzanne thought. This is too much for him especially after just getting out of his hospital bed today.

"That Robert is a fine boy." Tommy repeated, now less strident, more like he was talking to himself. "A real leader."

"Have you ever regretted adopting him?" Bronwen asked Jewell.

Adopted? Suzanne hid her surprise. Maybe that's why Robert hesitated telling his mother because he thought she might assume he was gay because of the way she raised him.

"No, no regrets, not for a second. Why would you ask such a thing?" Jewell said.

"Your own children came along, and then... well, I just wondered."

"Bronwen, you of all people know how much we wanted a child. He's been a blessing. You see what a fine young man he is. What are you thinking?"

"After he turned out to be, you know, I wondered if... Well, I thought maybe... John says he's sure it's not how they're raised, but I'm not sure. I always thought it was, but John says it's not and that I have misjudged the situation."

Jewell turned to Ed, looking puzzled. He coughed and squirmed in his seat.

John looked down and then whispered to Bronwen. "I don't think Robert told her yet."

"Told me what?" Jewell looked at one and then the other.

Tommy opened his eyes. "Told what?"

Ed stood and offered his hand to Jewell. "Let's go home and talk to Robert."

Jewell looked terrified. "Is he sick? Is something wrong?"

"No, no, nothing like that," Ed said. "Come on. He's been wanting to talk to you about something."

\* \* \*

Suzanne stayed by herself at the hospital that first night, relieved not to have to entertain other people, not that she had done that all day, but when they were around she felt like she should and then felt guilty when she didn't. She wrapped up in the blanket and rested on the couch. She drowsily considered her responsibilities to see if she had forgotten anything. Peter is in good hands, and they will call me if he wakes up. O Lord, let your Holy Spirit hold him. Julie is with the Edwards family. She'll be okay there. Jewell and Ed will be sensitive to her even though Jewell is digesting the news about Robert. Bell is probably sleeping like a rock at Bronwen and John's house. Not much keeps him awake. Liz is taking care of the congregation's needs. Bell's secretary will do the same in Salina. Or did he call anyone there? I'd better remind him of that tomorrow. I've talked to Mother and Dad and Frances. Frances will call our Columbus church. All my sisters know what's going on. Rebecca is keeping them informed. Sunday? What about Sunday? I'll have time while I wait here to plan the service and write a sermon. No, I can't do that. This is a time that people will understand if someone else takes care of that. Or maybe it will be another mark against me. This may be the best time to leave. It won't look like they ran me off.

In the middle of the night Suzanne turned around on the couch and punched her pillow for the hundredth time, but her eyes wouldn't stay shut. She saw the door open. Anna crept over and whispered. "Are you able to sleep?" she asked.

"Oh, Anna. No, I don't expect to sleep tonight. What are you doing up so late?"

"I couldn't stop thinking about you," she said sitting down next to

215

Suzanne. "Liz gave me an update on Peter, but I'm wondering how you are. Do you want company?"

"Yes," Suzanne said, thinking, not just any company, but yours is most welcome. "People have been very kind. It's surprising though that some of the very ones I thought were trying to get rid of me came and stayed most of the day."

"Liz said Brownen and John were here—and Tommy. Now there's a complicated man. I hardly recognize the boy I knew in high school. When we try to talk these days, I find we have nothing in common. And he can go from a gentle soul to a strident one in seconds."

"Do you think he'll use this to shoot another arrow at me?"

"I don't think so. It doesn't surprise me a bit that he was here," Anna said. "We fuss and disagree with each other like most families do, but when someone in the family is in trouble, everybody gathers round to help. It's an indication that you are part of the family. And that doesn't always happen with pastors."

Just before dawn a nurse came in. "Mrs. Hawkins, Peter is calling for you."

# CHAPTER 37

L ONG days and nights lost their definition. Dates didn't matter. Even Sundays failed to hold the power of the looming sermon deadline. A steady stream of visitors offered their hugs, prayers, food and magazines. Clergy from Middletown and even some from Salina came to the hospital and prayed with them. Suzanne and Bell alternated sleeping at Bronwen and John's, one of them always available to Peter. The Presbytery staff covered Sunday duties and pastoral care for Middletown and Salina First churches. Suzanne made hospital calls on parishioners who were admitted upstairs from the waiting room where she had established herself. The church secretaries phoned Suzanne and Bell every day to keep them informed and to get updates to pass on to parishioners. Jewell and Sarah kept Julie busy.

After the first calling out for his mother which only the nurse heard, it was another twenty-four hours before he did so again. Then he began responding slowly but steadily. Family and friends celebrated every sign of progress, but never spoke of the underlying question: What won't come back to him? After two weeks of tests, observation, and medications, he was released to go home and scheduled for more tests and appointments.

Suzanne was relieved to get him home, to observe him carefully and take care of him herself. She wanted them to get back to something closer to normal. However, she was a little nervous, wondering if she'd know how to handle every circumstance of his recovery.

Her sister Rebecca came for a week to help. "Now y'all settle down," she said. "Don't you worry about a thing. Julie and I have the meals planned, and we've bought all the groceries you're going to need for a good long while.

We'll figure out the best way to get Peter set up, and we'll go over everything the doctor told us. You're going to be just fine."

* * *

Tommy was admitted to the hospital again before Peter went home. Suzanne saw him every day and listened to him complain about the hospital, the doctor, the nurses. His foot was infected again, diabetes complicating his ability to heal. His fear became reality. The leg had to be amputated above the knee. He would not be comforted. Mary took him home and tried to care for him, but after a month, the foot on his other leg became infected and wouldn't heal. Eventually, that foot had to be taken. In September that year he went to live at the Presbyterian Manor care facility.

* * *

At home, Peter's headaches came and went. Dizziness and moments when words wouldn't come to him left him frustrated. A nurse came on Sundays to stay with him while Suzanne and Bell led worship. And Julie was his constant companion, playing games and watching television. The two churches generously agreed that their pastors could have office hours from home, doing as much as they could over the phone. Administration was difficult, but with the help of the church secretaries, the incessant mail, reports, record keeping and other details were handled or put on hold until they were in their offices. Suzanne went in on Sundays and Mondays. Bell went Sundays and Tuesdays.

Mildred called Suzanne every day to get the latest news and pass on her dubitable information. She reported that she visited Tommy every day and he didn't want anyone else to see him like he was. "He's even wearing diapers," she whispered.

Suzanne came to love Jewell as though she were a sister. Not only did she care for Julie, giving her a home when she went to work with Suzanne, she also counseled her wisely and made sure she had some fun, too.

One day when Suzanne was in the office, Jewell stopped in. "I didn't know Robert was gay," she said, "until that night at the hospital. We went home and had a long, long talk. Of course, I don't love Robert any less, but I grieve over the difficult life he will have. There are no easy choices.

Choices! How could anyone think a person would choose to be gay? I'm sure it's inborn. But it can't be genetic, can it? We'd see gay-ness in other generations. What do you think, Suzanne?"

"It certainly isn't an easy question or someone would have figured it out by now. But I agree it seems like we'd see patterns in families if it were genetic or for that matter if it were due to the way a person was raised. I hear of a gay gene, but I don't think that means it's passed down in the family."

"That's what Robert was most concerned about, that I not think the way I raised him was responsible. And now I know why Bronwen became so distant. She knew he was gay and blamed me. I don't know if we can ever be close again, but I hope so."

"Do you have any doubts about the way you raised him?"

"No, not really. I just wonder why. Why Robert?"

They were silent. There were no answers.

Jewell grimaced. "I heard somebody on the radio say that a gay person is an abomination to God."

Suzanne gasped. "What a terrible thing to say. That is not true at all. People may differ in how they read the Bible concerning homosexuality, but I will stand on the street corner and proclaim that what you heard—that abomination word—it's not true. It's not true! We know God loves Robert. I'm as sure of that as anything I know. And Robert is a good person. He's been a tremendous blessing to the young people in this church including Peter. If anybody says that word to you, let me know. I'll give them a piece of my mind."

# CHAPTER 38

DESPITE Mildred's caution that Tommy didn't want her to visit, Suzanne did go see him once a week. He met her with either angry talk about the nursing home or with a stoic face.

One day Helen, the director of the Presbyterian Manor called Suzanne. "I thought you should know," she said. "We can't keep The Colonel any longer. He's too out of control."

"What's happening?"

"He hit one of the aides yesterday and gave her a black eye. We're going to transfer him to the State Hospital in Topeka."

"Oh, no, Helen," Suzanne said. "Would you let me see if I can do anything to help before taking such a drastic action?"

The woman paused and breathed out noisily. "Oh, I don't know. We've tried everything, and I can't afford to have someone sue us. If he hits again, I'll be liable."

"I understand, I understand. I'll be right over to talk with him."

"Good. I haven't told him yet. It might help if you're here when I do."

* * *

"So, either you control your anger or you go to the State Hospital." Helen said. "No nursing home will take a violent patient, and I'm taking a huge risk to let you stay another minute. With the help of Mildred and your church, we're going to try one more time. But any sign of violence and you'll have to go." Having delivered her ultimatum, she gave Suzanne a nod and left.

Tommy's eyes held fear, perhaps better defined as terror. She had never seen that in him before. Pride, grief, tears, anger, concern, but never, ever fear. Surely though in his war service he'd felt fear, probably even come face to face with death. When Catherine died, Suzanne recalled he melted at the funeral home, but the rest of the time his face maintained its stoic mask. And in the time since, he might have been wearing a suit of armor for the little emotion that showed through except at the hospital waiting for Peter to wake up when they talked about Rose. Now, those huge eyes in his oversized face fell back in his head as he faced his last vestiges of power and dignity. She had seen the beginning of this when he lost one leg and then the other. Wearing diapers surely didn't help either. That hard shell of a face, which could dominate and intimidate, now drooped into purple bags under his eyes and flabby cheeks and jowls.

"Tommy, how can I help," Suzanne asked. She pulled a chair up to the side of his bed. He slumped down in bed no longer towering over her.

"There is no help for me. I wish I could just go on and die," he whispered.

She sat in silence. No words came to her. What can I say? God, what help will you give this man?

"I am going to hell."

"You don't have to leave here if you can control that anger."

"I'm going to die and go to hell."

"Tommy, is it that bad?" She'd heard confessions of men who still bore emotional wounds of what they had done during wartime. Perhaps as he lay here thinking about his deteriorating life, he felt the guilt of war.

"I've done a terrible thing."

"There is nothing God won't forgive."

"He won't forgive this."

"God wants you close to him. He wants to take away whatever stands in the way of that. If you truly are sorry and ask for forgiveness, it will be yours."

He closed his eyes and turned his head away. After a long silence, she left quietly.

* * *

It didn't take Mildred long to marshal the forces. She made sure someone was with Tommy all the time, to try to prevent further outbursts. Mary stayed all night and Mildred's team covered days.

Tommy ordered and then pleaded with Suzanne, "Get these women away from me. I want to be alone."

"It's the only way they'll let you stay," she told him.

* * *

He declined rapidly, not even wanting to sit up. He slipped further down into the bed.

Suzanne prayed with him every time she visited. One day they were alone, and she prayed specifically for his release from guilt and for his acceptance of forgiveness. "God of all Grace and Glory, you've known us all the days our lives. You know the days we've come close to being what you hoped we'd be and the days we haven't come close to that. Tommy has regrets, too heavy to bear, and he doesn't have hope that he can lay them down at your feet. Lord, grant him a ride on my faith and hope. He needs you. Jesus told us to ask you to forgive us as we forgive others, and so we do. I ask on his behalf, for he is obviously truly sorry and wants to be closer to you. Give him peace now and serenity in the days to come."

"Some things can't be forgiven," he whispered.

"You've said that before, but saying it doesn't make it true. You're wrong."

"How?"

"Confess and ask to be let off the hook."

After a long pause, he finally broke his silence again. "How?"

"Tell God what you have done and ask to be forgiven."

He took a deep breath, coughed, and tried to sit up in bed. Suzanne helped him get the pillows just right, and he began talking without looking at her, his chin on his chest.

"I did a terrible thing."

Suzanne moved her chair closer in order to hear him.

"Rose. She liked to work with me in the shop. She stayed out at the lake with Catherine and me in the summers. Such a beautiful girl." He shook his head. "Purity, innocence, a child at heart. She didn't know how to live in an adult body. When she was a child, everyone liked how affectionate she was. She'd hug and kiss. When she got older, she'd rub up against people in a bothersome way. She didn't know how to hold back on that, and nothing we could say got through to her. That day—." His voice broke. "I-I shoved her away. She fell and hit her head." He sobbed one quick gasp, like a man about to drown. "She was only fourteen. It was all my fault."

Mildred burst into the room carrying a plate of cookies and a huge bouquet of sunflowers. "Hey, sweetie. I'm here to cheer you up."

"Hi, Mildred," Suzanne said. "Beautiful flowers. We need a few more minutes to talk, actually about an hour. Would you come back later?"

"Oh, okay." She was visibly hurt, that lower lip jutting out like a child's.

"I'll stay until you get back. Maybe you could find a really big vase for those flowers."

It took a while for him to begin again. Suzanne sat quietly with her eyes closed, waiting, feeling peaceful, knowing that now he might find relief from his sins.

"She turned up pregnant at thirteen. Bronwen had been driving her to Topeka every day to a special school, and she became infatuated with the boys there. Nobody knew. We kept her at the lake that summer to prevent rumors, to keep her name and her family's reputation clean. The baby was adopted out.

"After that she kept telling me we were going to go find the baby and we'd build a house and get married – talking wild like that. I was afraid someone would hear her. Then that day... she was talking that way and—and that's when I pushed her away and she hit her head. Only fourteen. She wasn't to blame. She didn't know any better, a pure heart.

"I don't know how it happened. Don't know how I could have lost control. But you see I... no, no excuses. There is no excuse for it. And now, I'd do anything to take it back. If I could have that moment to live over, everything would be different. Robert is such a good boy, but look what he's become. The sins of the fathers are visited on the children." He bent his head into a towel and the tears flowed.

Suzanne put her hand on his and he didn't move away. Her brain clicked and beeped like a computer as it sorted and placed details in order. "Robert?" she asked.

Tommy nodded. Now his eyes searched hers.

"Sins of the fathers visited on the children?"

He nodded. "I sinned against God and God has brought this on Robert. And he's an abomination to God."

Suzanne caught her breath. "Surely you don't think that! You know that young man. He is a marvelous person."

"But he's, he's... you know."

"You think homosexuality is a sin?"

"Yes, it's abnormal."

"Many of us believe that a person is born a homosexual or heterosexual and that it isn't a choice."

"Yes, but what they do... It's not normal."

"Try thinking about it this way: there is great joy in loving another person, male or female. And having a partner to whom you are committed is a blessing. Focus on that and see if it makes any difference."

"As for your sin, is there anything you need to put right?"

"I can't undo it."

"No, but is there some way God can work with you to weave this into something good?"

Suzanne waited, letting the silence hold.

"Yoohoo, I'm back." Mildred carried in a three-foot high vase and set it down near the door. The sunflowers stood half way up the wall. "There you'll be able to see them from your bed."

# CHAPTER 39

LATE one rainy afternoon Suzanne reached Robert at home, picked him up and drove to the hospital.

"Why does the Colonel want to see me?" he asked.

"Let's get over there and find out."

\* \* \*

Tommy sat up tall in the bed, unusual of late. He had taken to sinking down under the sheet and sleeping most of the time when she visited. Now his curly black hair, streaked with grey, curled neatly back from his forehead, and he wore a white shirt with a red tie. Under his white, bushy eyebrows, his drooping eyes showed his fatigue.

Suzanne sat in a chair near the door and let Robert take the one next to the bed.

Without any preliminary conversation, Tommy asked Robert, "Do you like the cabin?"

"Yes, yes, sir, we all enjoy it. It's very generous of you to—."

Tommy cut him off. "That's not what I meant."

Robert waited. The young man's poise amazed Suzanne once again. He had amazing maturity for a nineteen-year-old boy. She felt certain he was strong enough to bear well the knowledge he was about to get.

Finally Tommy spoke again. "You know Rose died there."

"Yes, Mom and Dad have told me a lot about her."

"She was a very special young woman. Such a tragedy that she died so young and you couldn't know her. Robert, do you mind that you're adopted?"

"Mind?"

"Yes, have you ever been angry that you were given away and left to be raised by someone else?"

"No, not angry. Curious, though. Why, are you adopted, too?"

"No, just wondering." He coughed and took a long drink from the water glass by his bed.

"I know who they are," Tommy said. Robert looked puzzled. "Your real parents."

"You do? Are you going to tell me? But I guess you'd have to get their permission first, wouldn't you?"

"Are you ready to know?"

"I guess so. I know my real parents are Mom and Dad, and I wouldn't do anything to hurt them. But I don't think they'd mind. Are they ready to meet me?"

Tommy looked at Suzanne and she nodded. He took a deep breath. "Rose was your mother."

"Rose?" He wrinkled his forehead. "But wasn't she only fourteen when she died?"

Tommy nodded.

Robert looked down at his hands. His eyes moved back and forth as though he were reading a book. "Then that means my grandparents are Dr. John and Mrs. Lewis?"

Tommy nodded again.

"And you... you're my uncle?"

Tommy coughed several times and grimaced. "And your father. I'm your father." Then he coughed so hard and so long, Suzanne started to get up to help him, but Robert jumped quickly to support his back and hold him up until it was over.

"I need to—." Robert pointed to the door. "Excuse me."

Suzanne sat down in the chair he left but said nothing. After an initial moment of shock, her thoughts jumped around. It feels like a holy moment, but that's strange since the profane has been let loose in the room. No wonder he's weighed down with guilt. How could he have done such a thing? He's right. There is no excuse for it.

"Nobody else knows," he said to Suzanne. She sat beside his bed staring at her hands. There were no words.

Robert was gone so long she began to think he wouldn't come back. What shall I say to this man? I can't just leave now that he's confessed. If I do he'll no doubt take it as rejection and abandonment—from me and from God, too. I need to get ahold of myself. All have sinned and fallen short of the grace of God.

Tommy must have dropped off to sleep because he jumped when Robert stormed back in and stood at the end of the bed. "Why didn't anyone tell me? I never had any grandparents and I wanted them so much. And you don't know anything about me. Why wouldn't you want to? All this time..."

"I've been watching from afar. And Bronwen was real close to your mother when you were a baby," Tommy said.

"I remember that. Mother was really hurt when she stopped talking to her. Do you know what that's all about?"

Suzanne looked up to the ceiling. Little dove, we sure could use a fly over.

"I didn't want to hurt you or anybody in the family. That kind of stain stays with a family for years. Nobody knows that you're Rose's son except your parents and us. We protected Rose's memory. Nobody else knows Rose had a baby. Those who know she did, think some boy in that school in Topeka got her pregnant. I did a terrible thing. Ruined that pure love. In the end it killed her. I couldn't tell anybody." Tears rolled down his face.

"What about me? This is my life. Didn't anybody consider that?

While you all were protecting yourselves, look at all I missed. The truth. My grandparents. You – I hardly know you."

"We're real proud of you, Robert. You're a fine young man. Ah, that is, except for um. . .

"What? Being homosexual?"

Tommy looked away. "Yes. That's one reason I wanted to talk with you. I have a lot of money and when I die, I will leave a big chunk to the church and some to my brother. And there will be enough to keep Mary comfortable wherever she wants to live. Everything else will go to you, enough that you never need to work if you don't want to.

"But I hope you will. It's good for a man to work. In fact, I'm thinking you should join the Air Force. They'd make a man out of you. Or you could go somewhere and get fixed."

"Fixed?"

"Tommy!" Suzanne cried out. She could see Robert holding back anger but his clenched hands and stiff back betrayed him. How could he not be angry? This is beyond offensive.

"Tommy," she said trying to sound calmer than she felt, "it's not like a disease or a broken bone. Attempts to 'fix' young men have left them terribly messed up. I don't think we can understand what it's like to be wired differently."

"That's what John says. Well, I'm leaving you everything anyway. You'll decide what to do with it. You seem to have a level head and good people around you to help make decisions." He sighed. "Do your best. You deserve more than I've given you. At least this is something."

"I don't want your money," Robert said. "I don't need your money. I need you. Don't you think I want to know all about your life? All I know is you were a Colonel in the Air Force."

"Well, about that, that's not exactly the case. You see, I was about your age when I became obsessed with dreams of flying. . ."

Suzanne slipped out the door. It was time for Mary to arrive for the evening shift and she wanted to caution her not to go in until Robert left.

# CHAPTER 40

Two weeks later. Suzanne sat with Robert, taking turns holding Tommy's hand and talking to him. He had stopped responding the night before. John and Bronwen came in after school, and later Ed and Jewell joined them. They took turns sitting with Tommy, walking in the hall, and going for drinks and snacks.

A little after midnight Robert woke Suzanne. She had fallen asleep on a waiting room couch. "He's gone," Robert said, and they went back to stand with the others and look down at The Colonel.

Suzanne prayed. "Gracious God. we offer this man back into your arms, praying for your mercy and your grace as we honor this holy moment."

No one except Suzanne and Robert knew that Tommy was Robert's father. And only the family knew Robert was Rose's biological son. Later, when the will was read, no one in the family acted surprised when they found out he'd left most of his estate to Robert. After all he was Rose's son and Tommy's nephew. Of course, people in the church and community didn't even know Rose had had a baby. Mildred asked lots of questions, but Suzanne feigned ignorance.

Robert sang at his funeral, the song Tommy had sung so many times. "When you think there's no bright tomorrow and you feel you can't try again, suddenly there's a valley where hope and love begin."

Robert and Suzanne had several long talks. He still had anger to express and deal with. And he worried about whether to tell his parents what he knew. Finally, he let them know Tommy had told him he was Rose's son. The rest he kept to himself. "It would do no one any good," he said.

* * *

Mary moved to Virginia. She told Suzanne, "The Colonel and Catherine gave me a good life, when it was doubtful I'd have had much of one in Virginia, but now I'm going home to get reacquainted with my brothers and sisters and their families. There's nothing for me here any more. Nobody needs me. And the Colonel was quite generous. I won't have to work any more."

Bronwen and Jewell became friends again, though their differences on homosexuality still cast a shadow. When Bronwen confessed to Jewell that she no longer thought Robert's homosexuality was due to the way he'd been raised, she also admitted that she had been afraid there was something about Rose that had led to him being "that way."

* * *

Peter begged the doctor to let him start school when the other kids did. And with some warnings and promises, the doctor agreed. "You may not play any sports, not even ride your bike yet. Avoid anything that puts you in danger of hitting your head. Another injury could be disastrous. Get nine hours of sleep at night and report anything unusual."

When his math teacher noticed that he didn't respond when she called on him, she phoned Bell. "He seems to go into a staring daze sometimes."

This led to more tests. The doctor prescribed regular brain scans and tried several prescriptions to reduce what they found were seizures.

Suzanne still worried about him because he wasn't rude to her any more.

He started taking guitar lessons and displayed a more peaceful emotional life. She would have given anything to have the real him back. But she remembered to be grateful every day that he was alive and well.

* * *

When Suzanne met with the Presbytery's Committee on Ministry to debrief her time at Covenant Church, she looked around at the other pastors and elders representing area churches and hoped they would understand her failure to complete the interim work.

The moderator Jan began. "Rev. Hawkins met with us in January for a three month check up. We cancelled the April meeting with her since we had such a full agenda, and we've waited until now to give her time to get her feet back under her after her son had a head injury. You'll remember we've been praying for Peter. Suzanne, will you remind us what you covered in January and then bring us up to date?"

"Certainly," Suzanne began. "At the beginning I made it a priority to get to know them individually and as a whole congregation. I helped the Session update their personnel policies and administrative manual. We reviewed their financial management procedures, which needed very little modification. When a minor conflict arose, I taught them the levels of conflict and discussed how to keep matters at the level of a problem to solve. The most difficult time for me personally came when rumors began spreading about me and a member of the congregation. I know Sadie has reported to you how we handled that. I think the open discussion of gossip helped. I became aware of some long time patterns in the congregation. Two individuals in particular have histories that connect with the congregation in unhealthy ways. One of those has been resolved. The other—well, I guess all I can say is I've dealt with that, but time will tell how successfully.

"In the last few months I lost track of where the congregation stood and what interim tasks to do next. I think I became so much a part of the community that my objectivity flew out the window—even before Peter's head injury. Then when he had his accident, the people supported us and helped in every way. I kept up with congregational needs, but he was my main priority.

Recently, a long-time pillar of the church died. That will affect the church, but I'm not sure how much or in what ways. In summary, I don't think we've solved their dysfunction, but we have taken some steps. I'm sorry I haven't done more. I hope the next person can go further."

"How is Peter?" Sadie asked.

"He's doing very well with only a few remaining problems. He started school on time. We are very thankful."

"And, how are you doing?" a woman asked. "That's a lot of stress for one year. In fact, ever since you moved here, you've been dealing with major church difficulties."

"I'm tired," she said. "I'm very tired."

"Do you want to take some time off before starting another assignment?"

"Yes. That would be good. I think my family needs some extra care right now. We're going to have to watch Peter and hold him back from anything that could put him in danger of another head injury. And he needs extra rest. It won't be easy for him to follow the doctor's orders."

There were smiles around the table. "I don't envy you herding a teenage boy," one of the men said.

"Suzanne," Sadie said, forehead wrinkled and concern on her face, "I detect a note of regret in your voice, but I want to tell you that you have done an amazing job in the two churches you've served since coming here. You have strengthened the fainthearted, supported the weak, helped the afflicted, and honored everyone. You have loved and served the Lord. God bless you, my dear."

# CHAPTER 41

O N Suzanne's last Sunday, Mildred gave her strict instructions. "Don't go downstairs. Don't go to the kitchen. And if you forget, I have guards posted." She grinned, crinkling her eyes.

The head table sat at the far end of the fellowship hall with the round tables scattered nearby like they were at the welcoming dinner nearly a year earlier. It seemed much longer ago than that to Suzanne. Bronwen and John again sat with Suzanne, Bell, Peter and Julie. Now, they were family. And as she looked at the congregation gathered in eights around the tables, she thought of the feeding of the five thousand. Jesus had them sit in small groups, and there was enough food for all of them. Why am I thinking of that? she wondered. There is more than enough food here.

Mildred proudly presented Suzanne with an album of pictures interspersed with notes from individuals in the congregation. JJ gave her a beautifully framed picture of her in Welsh dress. "We expect you to come back on St. David's Day. I'll even let you wear my aunt's hat again," he said.

John and Bronwen showed everyone a formal portrait of her, which Ed had taken. "It will hang in the hallway outside the offices," John said. "We've run out of space in Mildred's history room so the Session has decided to begin a new wall of pictures of our pastors." In private he told Suzanne, "I don't know why this church has been so difficult in the past. I can't remember what that was like now. Everybody's getting along, I think we'll be okay."

I hope so, she thought. But I wonder how they will characterize me after I'm gone.

Morgan and Ralph handed her both babies and took her picture. They also gave her a basket of homegrown and homemade food and a photograph of her baptizing Julia and Miriam.

Ed Edwards gave Bell a huge dinner bell. "This is to add to the collection of Bell's bells. Keep it where you can call the family to come eat your cooking."

Representatives of the youth group and youth choir presented Julie and Peter with a collage for each of them. Each one held a composition of photos, messages, and some items Suzanne didn't understand the significance of. They filled the three foot square posters with color and energy. Robert and Jewell beamed at the work of their groups.

Tears fell down Suzanne's cheeks and mingled with those on cheeks of others as they hugged her and wished her well. "You will always be family to me," she said.

She had already told them as part of her last sermon, "I'll have to distance myself so you can welcome a new pastor and forge a new pastoral relationship. As much as I might want to, I won't be doing funerals, weddings, or baptisms. Get to know your new pastor." Still they would be family.

Sarah and Matt often joined Peter and Julie in Salina for weekend tornaments of table games. Suzanne kept a close watch on Peter.

She invited JJ to join them for Thanksgiving Dinner in Salina and welcomed him to come see them before then. And she made sure Jewell had the Harvest Church's Chicken Noodle Dinner on her calendar for December. They had talked about making that an annual tradition for their families along with opening the cottage in springtime.

Robert had several long talks with Suzanne before she left. He wanted her advice about how to use the money and the house Tommy had left him. "I want to do something meaningful with it. Something for people who need help." As they talked, he came up with a short list:

- Finding ways to help immigrants find housing
- Founding a shelter for abused women and children
- Providing college for Matthew and Sarah
- Establishing a trust for the church
- Building a new house for Mom and Dad

"I may build another room on the cabin or buy an RV to keep out there. Mom says she thinks Bronwen and John Lewis—or whatever I should call them—may go out to the cabin with us, and I want there to be room for all your family and all of us."

"It's possible that I can do all of that," he said. "He's left me way beyond any amount I could ever conceive of."

He struggled with having knowledge no one else had, and she didn't know how to advise him on that. "Robert, keeping family secrets can create increasing anxiety within a family system. But, I don't know about this. It seems on the surface it affects no one but you. Those closest to you know Rose was your mother, and you can talk to them about that. But telling anyone about Tommy... In the end it's going to be your decision. It seems to me that your knowing the truth is most important, as was Tommy's telling you. You were very generous to him, forgiving him enough that the two of you could get to know each other in his last weeks. However, you probably need to talk further about your birth mother and father, especially if you have any lingering anger. I know a good family therapist in Salina. You could trust her, and she'd be someone outside of Middletown to talk things through with."

He said he'd like to do that.

\* \* \*

Suzanne drove home alone after that last Sunday. The children had left with Bell earlier. She passed the meat processing plant and Hometown Bakery. When did I stop noticing the smells? she wondered. She wound around through the beautiful Flint Hills, which were covered in autumn browns and rusts. Ahead of her cows covered hills on both sides of the road. I still like the way they look, she thought, but I'll never tell Ralph and Morgan that, since they rue the loss of the natural prairie to grazing. She drove home toward the setting sun, relaxing in the rosy glow of twilight.